PICK AND ROLL

James Lorimer & Company Ltd., Publishers acknowledges the support of the Ontario Arts Council. We acknowledge the financial support of the Government of Canada through the Canada Book Fund for our publishing activities. We acknowledge the support of the Canada Council for the Arts which last year invested $24.3 million in writing and publishing throughout Canada. We acknowledge the Government of Ontario through the Ontario Media Development Corporation's Ontario Book Initiative.

Cover design: Meredith Bangay
Cover image: Shutterstock

Library and Archives Canada Cataloguing in Publication

Blair, Kelsey, author
 Pick and roll / Kelsey Blair.

(Sports stories)
Issued in print and electronic formats.
ISBN 978-1-4594-0601-8 (pbk.).--ISBN 978-1-4594-0602-5 (bound).--ISBN 978-1-4594-0603-2 (epub)

I. Title. II. Series: Sports stories (Toronto, Ont.)

PS8603.L3154P52 2014   jC813'.6   C2013-906821-X
C2013-906822-8

James Lorimer & Company Ltd.,	Distributed in the United States by:
Publishers	Orca Book Publishers
317 Adelaide Street West, Suite 1002	P.O. Box 468
Toronto, ON, Canada	Custer, WA USA
M5V 1P9	98240-0468
www.lorimer.ca	

Printed and bound in Canada.
Manufactured by Friesens Corporation in Altona, Manitoba, Canada in March 2014.
Job #201134

For my parents, Jim Blair and Joan Blair.
You are my home court advantage.

CONTENTS

1 GAME DAY

Seven-thirty in the morning. Ugh. Fourteen-year-old Jazz Smith-Mohapatra walks into the kitchen and yawns. She stretches her arms from side to side like she's trying to touch the walls.

"How can you be tired?" says Jazz's mom. She smiles as she bustles around the kitchen. "You just woke up."

"I never sleep well on game days," grumbles Jazz.

"Right!" says Jazz's dad as he rushes through the kitchen. "You've got a game tonight, don't you?"

"Last game of the regular season," says Jazz. The game is still hours away, but Jazz is already nervous.

"I've got to work," says Jazz's dad, "so I won't be able to make it. Good luck tonight!"

"Thanks," mumbles Jazz, trying to hide her disappointment.

"Enough about basketball," says Jazz's mom. "How is school going?"

"It's okay," answers Jazz. She doesn't want to think about school. She wants to think about basketball. Jazz's team, the Pipers, will be playing their cross-town grade nine rivals, the Hornets, for first place in Vancouver's high-school basketball league.

"Did you get your grade for the math test you took last week?"

Jazz vaguely remembers taking the test. She thinks she understood the questions at the beginning, but she struggled with the questions at the end. When the bell rang, Jazz was on the third-to-last question, but the teacher took her paper away before she could finish. Classes like history and English are all right, but even when she studies for hours, Jazz has never done better than a C on a math test.

"Not yet," answers Jazz.

"Tell me when you do. It's important that you work as hard in the classroom as you do on that basketball court."

"I know, Mom," says Jazz. Jazz packs her lunch and her pregame snack in her bag. She doesn't need to bring her own basketball, but she puts it in her bag anyway.

Jazz looks at herself in the full-length hallway mirror. She's wearing blue jeans and a tight-fitting emerald tank top that plays up her brown skin and hazel eyes. From the corner of her eye, Jazz sees a grey sweatshirt hanging in the hall closet. She stares at it for a long moment, but decides not to wear it.

"Cindy's in the driveway," announces Jazz's mom.

Jazz nods and goes outside to meet her best friend. She notices they are wearing almost the same outfit, but Cindy's tank top is bright pink. Cindy quickly looks her up and down before she pulls Jazz into an enthusiastic hug.

"Morning," says Jazz once Cindy has released her.

"You look awesome today," Cindy says, tossing her blonde hair.

"Thanks." Jazz wonders what Cindy would have said if she'd worn an outfit Cindy didn't like. Like that grey sweatshirt, for example.

"I have a surprise," announces Cindy brightly. As if she was reading Jazz's mind, she pulls a green and yellow sweatshirt out of her backpack. "Mom and I went shopping yesterday, and I saw this. Isn't it great? It's our team colours."

"It is," says Jazz, as Cindy slips her arms into the sleeves. Jazz knows that she could never wear those colours with bright pink, but somehow Cindy gets away with it.

"The best part is that Mom said I could get you one, too." Cindy pulls out a matching sweatshirt and hands it to Jazz.

"Thanks!" Jazz pauses. She thinks about the sweatshirt hanging in her closet. "But don't you hate it when people wear sweatshirts to school? You made fun of Ella for wearing one last week."

"But it looks cool when *we* do it."

"Whatever you say," says Jazz, putting on the sweatshirt.

"I'm so excited for the game tonight. Maybe they'll

give out a Most Valuable Player award if our team goes on to win the championship. Remember our first basketball camp?"

Jazz smiles at the memory. "We were seven, and the hoop looked so high. I thought I'd never be able to score a basket. I wanted to quit at the end of the first day."

"But I wouldn't let you."

"Because you said you wouldn't be my friend anymore if I quit," Jazz reminds Cindy.

"I didn't want to be there without you," Cindy admits. "Anyway, it totally worked out. They gave both of us the MVP award on the last day."

"Let's focus on tonight's game first. The Hornets are the best team in the league."

"Second best," corrects Cindy sharply. "No one is better than us."

"Ugh," says Jazz as they approach the math classroom. "I hope Mr. Maxwell doesn't check homework. I didn't have time to finish after practice last night."

"You can copy mine if you want," offers Cindy.

"Thanks, but I can't copy your homework every day."

"Why not? It's just math."

"Hi," says Brad from across the aisle as Jazz slides into her seat. His skin is chocolate brown. Dimples appear on his cheeks whenever he smiles, like he is doing now.

"Hi," replies Jazz shyly, looking down to open her

backpack. Her math notebook is at the bottom of her bag, and Jazz piles textbooks on her desk so she can reach it. Distracted by Brad's brown eyes, Jazz knocks one of the books off her desk and onto her left foot. "Ow!"

"You okay?" asks Brad.

"I'm fine."

"Smooth," whispers Cindy from her seat behind Jazz.

"Shut up," replies Jazz, blushing wildly.

"Are you two excited about the game tonight?" asks Brad.

"Totally," replies Cindy.

"Totally," agrees Jazz. "Maybe a little nervous, too."

"Why?" asks Cindy. "We're going to win tonight. Then we'll win all our playoff games and the championship. And Jazz and I will share the MVP award."

"That does sound pretty awesome," smiles Brad.

"Jazz is the leading scorer," breaks in a new voice. Jazz looks up to see Adam Ross on his way to his seat at the back of class.

"So?" challenges Cindy.

"She's also the best rebounder on the team, and she has the best shooting percentage."

"What does that mean?" asks Brad curiously. Brad is the star of the swim team, but doesn't know anything about team sports.

"Shooting percentage is calculated by —" Adam starts.

"I don't care how it's calculated," interrupts Brad. "What does it mean?"

"When a basketball player shoots the ball, she either scores or she doesn't. A high shooting percentage is a good thing. It means she scores lots of the shots that she takes."

"How do you know Jazz's shooting percentage?" asks Brad curiously.

"My friend Ella is on the team," answers Adam. "I like to keep track of statistics."

"So what?"

"In basketball, you can track different parts of the game by using math. For example, you might keep track of the number of points each player has scored or the number of minutes each player has played. You can keep track of statistics for one game or several games. I keep all the Pipers' statistics in my head. It's an interesting way to watch the game. Cindy, you are the team's fifth leading scorer, and you have a low shooting percentage." Finally, Adam stops to take a breath.

Cindy sits up straight in her chair. "So?"

"It is highly unlikely that you would share the Most Valuable Player award with Jazz. It is far more likely that Jazz would win the award by herself."

Cindy glares at Adam. Her stare is so fierce, Jazz is surprised Adam doesn't shiver with fear. Fortunately, before Cindy has the chance to say anything, Mr. Maxwell strides in and starts the class.

"I've marked last week's tests," Mr. Maxwell announces. "Some of you did great work." Mr. Maxwell scans the classroom. As he says the word "great," he looks in Jazz's direction. His eyes are warm and proud. Jazz is surprised, then happy, until she realizes that the teacher is looking at someone behind her. She slumps down in her seat. "Some of you need to keep working. We'll go over the answers as a group. If there's time left at the end, you can get started on today's homework assignment."

Thirty minutes later, Cindy taps Jazz on the shoulder. "That was so boring. I don't get why we have to go over the answers in class."

"I got ninety percent," agrees Brad's friend Jeremy. "So I already know the answers."

Jazz tucks the test paper into her backpack. She doesn't want anyone to know she got 59 percent. When Jazz looks up, Brad is watching her.

"I thought it was kind of helpful to go over stuff," says Brad, offering Jazz a smile. She wonders if he saw the mark on the top of her test. The last thing she wants is for Brad to think she's stupid.

"Whatever," says Cindy loudly. "Time for more important things." Cindy whips a bottle of bright yellow nail polish from her backpack.

"What's that for?" asks Brad.

"Jazz and I always have matching nails for the game."

Jazz looks at Cindy's nails, already yellow. It looks

like she stuck her fingertips in a bottle of mouldy mustard.

"I think I'll put my nail polish on after lunch," says Jazz. "I want to go to the gym."

"No way," answers Cindy. "You played basketball at lunch yesterday. And I want to do your nails."

"But I want to be ready for today's big game."

Cindy turns Brad. "Jazz has to eat with us. Right, Brad?"

"Right," says Brad, smiling widely. "Come on, Jazz. It'll be good to get your mind off the game."

"Oh, fine," says Jazz. "I'll eat lunch with you." She turns to Cindy. "Happy?"

"Very," says Cindy brightly. "Meet me in the lunch-room right when the lunch bell rings."

"I will."

"Promise?"

"Promise."

Cindy smiles and Jazz heads for her next class.

When the lunch bell rings, Jazz goes to the lunch-room to meet Cindy

"Hey Jazz," greets Jeremy from a nearby table, motioning for Jazz to join him.

"Have you seen Cindy?"

"Not since math." Jazz scans the cafeteria. Cindy isn't in the cafeteria line or sitting at another table. Jazz slips into the seat beside Jeremy. On the other side of the table, Jazz's teammate Marie is unpacking her lunch.

"I just got a pet hedgehog," announces Marie proudly. "His name is . . ." Jazz's attention drifts away from Marie and toward the doors. Still no sign of Cindy. "Isn't that awesome, Jazz?"

"What?"

"Harry."

"Harry?"

"My hedgehog."

"Oh yeah . . . he sounds great."

"He is. Maybe, I'll bring him to school one day."

"Great," replies Jazz. Why is Jazz talking about a hedgehog when she could be practicing basketball?

Twenty minutes later, Cindy and Brad walk into the lunchroom. Seeing Jazz, Cindy skips toward the table.

"Where have you been?" asks Jazz before Cindy has the chance to say hello.

"At my locker," replies Cindy dismissively. "Move over. Brad and I need to sit down."

"There's room on this side of the table," offers Marie.

"I need to sit beside Jazz. I'm painting her nails for tonight's game."

"Can you do mine after?"

"Maybe."

Reluctantly, Jeremy and Jazz move over to make room for Cindy. Jazz holds out her hand and lets Cindy paint her nails mouldy mustard yellow.

2 THE SCREEN

After school, Jazz stands in front of the mirror in the locker room, wearing her green and yellow jersey with the number 12 on the front. She has already eaten her regular pregame meal: a cucumber and cream cheese sandwich. Jazz runs her fingers through her long, black hair exactly ten times. On the tenth time, she flips her head back. Her hair flies everywhere and she catches the loose strands in her fingers. She twists her wrist until all of her hair is held back in a tight ponytail. Perfect.

Jazz takes a deep breath. It's a big game.

Cindy walks in and stands beside Jazz. "This jersey makes me look like a colour-blind clown."

Jazz looks at their matching uniforms. "That's not true," she says seriously. "The green makes you look like more like a leprechaun than a clown." Cindy's jaw drops, and Jazz laughs. "I'm only kidding. You always look good."

"Of course I do."

"What do you think Coach Chan will do when we

win tonight?" asks Cindy as she ties up her hair.

"We haven't won yet."

"We will."

As Cindy walks away, Jazz puts headphones in her ears. She closes her eyes and listens to the beat of her pre-game playlist. Jazz peeks out the locker-room door. The gym is packed with grade nine students and their parents. Jazz doesn't bother looking for her parents in the stands. She closes the door.

Jazz's fingers tingle with nerves, and she shakes out her hands. The Hornets and the Pipers are fierce rivals. Whoever wins this game will play against the weakest team in the first round of playoffs. In playoffs, every advantage helps.

Cindy stands, snapping her fingers over her head, and everyone looks up at her. "I'm having an end-of-regular-season party at my house on Saturday. You're all invited." She pauses and turns to Ella, the Pipers" starting point guard. "Yes, even you, Ella."

Ella blushes. Unlike Cindy and Jazz, Ella is short and thin, and her facial features are small and mouse-like. Cindy always tells Jazz that it is Ella's own fault that she's so desperately, terribly, horribly unpopular. At school, Ella spends most of her time in the library, and she only has one friend — know-it-all Adam Ross. There is no one in the world more annoying than Adam Ross, and anyone who is friends with him is a loser. At least, that's what Cindy says.

Pick and Roll

Coach Chan walks in for their pregame talk. Jazz listens to his strategy, bouncing her knee up and down nervously. When Coach Chan finally stops talking, Jazz is relieved. She's ready to get on the court and warm up.

As Jazz dribbles the ball in warm-up, her nerves begin to settle. The feel of the basketball against her palm is calming. By the time warm-up is finished, Jazz's mind is clear and her body is ready.

Jazz jumps up and down on the spot as Coach Chan reads the starting lineup. There is no point in listening, since the starters have been the same all season. Ella plays point guard, calling the plays. Along with her are Cindy, Ashley, Jazz, and Joanne, who is the tallest girl in grade nine.

"Brad is here," whispers Cindy to Jazz. Jazz glances into the stands where Brad sits with Jeremy. "If you play well, I'll bet he asks you out."

Usually Jazz would be excited to see Brad in the gym. But it's too close to the start of the game, and Jazz simply nods at Cindy.

As usual, Joanne stands ready to take the tipoff that starts the game at centre court. She squares off across from the Hornets' tallest player, ready to tap the ball to a teammate. Jazz takes a step to the left to get in the best position for Joanne to tip her the ball. The referee blows her whistle and tosses ball into the air.

From the moment Joanne wins the tipoff, the game is fast and intense. It is the perfect style of play for Jazz.

She is a physical player and likes to make contact with the player she is defending. Nothing makes Jazz feel more powerful than jumping into the air and grabbing a rebound.

The second time down the court, Ella calls the play, *"Up!"*

Defended by Hornets' Number 14, Jazz stands on the side of the rectangular key farthest from the basket. Cindy makes a move and gets open on one side of the court, near the sideline. Ella starts the play by passing Cindy the ball. As soon as the ball leaves Ella's hands, she runs past Jazz toward the basket. Jazz waits for Ella to go by, then moves toward Cindy. She plants her feet firmly on the ground and crosses her arms over her chest to make a screen. Cindy will dribble the ball past Jazz to the basket to try to score. If the play works, the Hornets' player defending Cindy will run into Jazz. Jazz keeps her feet planted and waits for Cindy to move.

"Screen right," yells Jazz's defender to warn her teammate. "Screen coming on your right!"

The Hornets' player defending Cindy hears the warning, but it's too late. Cindy brushes past Jazz's shoulder on her way to the basket. Her defender runs into Jazz with a *thump*. As Cindy shoots the ball, one of the Hornets slaps her wrist. The referee sees the slap and blows her whistle to call the a foul. But Jazz keeps her eye on the ball. It circles around the hoop and falls through the mesh of the basket.

"Yeah!" shouts Jazz triumphantly.

The crowd cheers loudly, and Jazz gives Cindy a high-five. Being the first team on the scoreboard is always a good way start to a game.

By the fourth quarter, players on both teams sweat as they sprint up and down the court. The score is 52–50 for the Hornets.

Most of the Hornets' points have been scored by their best player, Catherine Hugh. Joanne is defending Catherine, but Catherine is even taller than the tallest Pipers' player, and she is very skilled. Any time Catherine touches the ball, she scores.

Jazz jostles with her defender for position close to the basket.

The Hornets' Number 14 turns to the referee on the baseline. "Ref, she's got her hands all over me!"

With a whistle in her mouth, the referee responds. "Hands off, Number 12."

Jazz takes her hands off Number 14's body, but keeps their hips connected.

Number 14 huffs in frustration. "Stop pushing me!"

Jazz manages to force Number 14 out of position. But the Hornets' star player gets the ball on the other side of the basket and makes a strong move. Catherine scores again. Coach Chan calls a timeout.

The Pipers gather around their coach. "Guys —" he starts.

"*Girls*," mutters Ella.

Coach Chan rolls his eyes. "*Girls*, we're getting out-muscled. You need stand your ground. Get physical. They're playing a rough game and we need to match that intensity." The team nods. "We've got the ball out of bounds on the sideline. Ella, what play should we run?"

"*Chop*," says Ella quietly. It's a play that has her passing the ball from out of bounds. A Pipers' player has to set a screen to free a teammate from her defender in the five seconds Ella has to pass the ball.

"*Chop* it is. I want Jazz setting the screen. She's our toughest player."

"That's for sure," says Joanne nervously. "Did you see her rebound last play?" She turns to Jazz. "You practically jumped on top of the girl to get the ball."

"She did what she had to do," replies Coach Chan. "If the ref doesn't call it, it isn't a foul."

The horn sounds to signal the end of the timeout. Jazz takes her position at the top of the key. She looks into the stands. All eyes are on the court. Every second matters. Every rebound matters. Every screen matters. Jazz feels the energy in the gym swell.

Joanne shifts her weight to the balls of her feet so that she's ready to move when the play begins. Catherine is defending her. Just before the referee hands Ella the ball, Jazz sees Catherine discreetly elbow Joanne in the stomach.

No one elbows my teammate and gets away with it, Jazz thinks. She prepares to set a hard screen.

Ella takes the ball from the referee and slaps it. Joanne fakes hard toward Ella, as if she wants the ball. Catherine believes the fake and lunges forward. With Catherine off balance, Joanne has the advantage. Jazz runs to her spot and sets her feet on the ground. Desperate to recover position, Catherine doesn't see Jazz's screen and sprints to follow Joanne.

Hearing the Pipers' fans cheer them on, Jazz crosses her arms over her chest and braces herself for the contact.

As Catherine collides with her, Jazz feels a surge of pride. This screen is bound to help Joanne get open under the basket. And it'll teach the Hornets' player not to elbow one of Jazz's teammates.

But as Catherine slams into Jazz's crossed arms, her neck whips forward and back. Her head slams into Jazz's shoulder, and the sound of thud echoes in Jazz's ears.

The gym goes silent.

Jazz looks down and her stomach drops. In front of Jazz's feet, Catherine lies on the court, completely still.

3 CONSEQUENCES

Later in her bedroom, Jazz replays the screen over and over in her mind. Ella slapped the ball. Joanne faked toward the sideline, and then Jazz moved. Jazz remembers jumping into place. Her feet felt solid on the hardwood of the court. She knew it was going to be a good screen. Jazz didn't move her feet or extend her arms. She simply stood. And Catherine hit her.

At least, that's what Jazz *thinks* happened. It wasn't what the referee thought happened when she ejected Jazz from the game. It wasn't what the team thought happened when they walked into the locker room, shooting nervous looks at Jazz. Everyone else seems to think Jazz set an unfair screen on purpose. They think she intended to hurt Catherine.

Jazz jumps up and turns on her stereo. Silence reminds Jazz of the eerie quiet that filled the gym when Catherine hit the ground. Standing on the court, Catherine was big and strong. But lying on the ground, she looked fragile. She looked broken.

"How can you be listening to music?" demands Jazz's mother. She stands at the doorway of Jazz's room, her hands on her hips.

Jazz looks to the ground. "It was too quiet."

Jazz's mom shuts off the stereo. "Silence makes you think, and you need to think about what you did."

"I didn't mean for Catherine to get hurt."

"That isn't what I heard from Coach Chan. He says you were pushing Number 14 all game."

"She was pushing me, too."

"That makes it right? What kind of daughter have I raised?"

"It's part of the game."

"Maybe it is, but it's part of the game your father and I do not like. Why couldn't you have picked a nice sport? Like gymnastics?"

"I can't even touch my toes."

"If you'd joined gymnastics, you'd be able to. But it doesn't matter now. Tonight is a school night, and it's time for you to go to bed."

Her mom leaves and Jazz checks her phone for what seems like the hundredth time. Cindy hasn't replied to any of Jazz's calls or text messages.

Jazz curls up in bed. Every time she closes her eyes, she's flooded with memories from the game and all the talk afterward. Without Catherine playing for the Hornets, the Pipers won the game by two points. But Coach Chan said that Catherine probably has a concussion. The doctors will know more the next day, but it is unlikely Catherine will be able to play in playoffs. She might even have to take a long break from basketball.

Jazz shivers. She can't imagine what she'd do without basketball in her life. When she thinks about Catherine sitting on the sidelines, it makes her feel like she's going to throw up.

After several hours of tossing and turning in bed, Jazz gets up and flips on the light switch. She lowers herself onto her stomach and wriggles her way under her bed. The bed frame rubs against her shoulders, but Jazz persists, reaching her right hand toward the wall. Finally, she feels what she's looking for. Jazz pulls out Winston, a stuffed moose. Cindy gave her Winston for Christmas the first year they were friends. Jazz turns off the light and crawls back under the covers, holding Winston tightly to her chest.

★★★

After an awful night's sleep, Jazz sits in English class and taps her mustard-yellow fingernails on her desk. She hasn't seen or spoken to Cindy. It feels like everyone is watching her.

"Would Jazz Smith-Mohapatra please report to the principal's office," says a voice over the speaker system.

Mrs. Moller, the English teacher, nods at Jazz. "You may go. Take your bag with you."

Jazz stuffs her notebook into her backpack and walks down to the office. Coach Chan waits in the hall-way outside the office.

"What's going on?" asks Jazz.

"The Hornets have submitted a complaint to the league about your screen."

"What does that mean?"

"It means they're being ridiculous! You didn't do anything wrong. You're just a tough player who set a hard screen."

"Are you sure?"

"Of course I am." Coach Chan leads Jazz to the principal's office.

"Please take a seat," says Ms. Calerone, waving at a couple of chairs.

Jazz feels as if she's about to play the biggest game of her life. Her heart is thumping in her chest. She sits in one of the uncomfortable chairs across from the principal's desk.

"You had a big game last night," says Ms. Calerone.

"Yeah . . ." begins Jazz. *Where is this going?* she wonders.

"I have already spoken to your parents. They thought it would be best if Coach Chan and I updated you."

"About what?"

Coach Chan turns to Jazz. "Catherine Hugh went to the hospital last night. The doctors think she has a third-grade concussion. Do you know what that means?"

"That her head got badly shaken up?"

"That's more or less right," answers Ms. Calerone. "It's a serious injury. She'll have to sit out the rest of season, and she won't be able to play for at least three months. There may also be long-term effects. Catherine might have problems with her memory and have trouble sleeping. And she might experience depression or develop depression later in life."

Jazz's stomach drops, and she can feel her eyes become heavy with tears.

"Those things may not happen," says the principal, seeing Jazz's face. "It's too early to know for sure."

There is a long silence. Jazz tries to hold back her tears, but it's no use. They begin to flow down her cheeks.

"The Hornets have put in a complaint with the league," says Coach Chan.

"They think I hurt Catherine on purpose, don't they?" mumbles Jazz through her tears.

"Did you?" asks Ms. Calerone.

"No."

"Obviously, you didn't mean for her to get hurt so badly. From what I hear it was an intense game. Very physical. You have the reputation for being an aggressive player. Maybe you accidentally got carried away?"

"No!" Jazz blurts out. She suddenly remembers

seeing Catherine elbow Joanne ribs. She remembers thinking Catherine should pay for it.

"There's no need to yell," cautions Coach Chan. He turns to Ms. Calerone. "But Jazz is right. She didn't do anything wrong."

"We aren't trying to blame anyone. We're just trying to figure out what happened. That's why the Vancouver High School Basketball League has set up a hearing with the Fair Play Commission. Catherine's dad recorded the game. They're going to look at the video and decide what to do."

"What to do?"

"Whether or not you'll be allowed to play in the playoffs. And whether or not you'll be allowed to play next year."

"What?" Jazz can't believe what she's hearing. She thinks about what school would be like if she wasn't allowed be a member of the basketball team. No teammates. No adrenaline rush from grabbing a rebound in a close game. Nothing to look forward to during math class.

"She's my best player," says Coach Chan forcefully. "The Hornets are just trying to take her out of the game so they can win the championship title."

"I'm sure that's not true," replies Ms. Calerone sternly. "Because the referee ejected you from the game, you are already suspended for one game. You will have to miss the first round of playoffs, no matter what. The hearing will decide whether or not to extend the suspension though playoffs or into next year."

"Next year?" What would she do without basketball for that long?

"Don't worry yet," says Ms. Calerone. "The Fair Play Commission will look at the tape. They may decide the screen you set was fair, and you'll be able to play in the second round of playoffs. Because playoffs are soon, I've managed to convince the committee to hold the hearing tomorrow.

Jazz doesn't know what to say, so she doesn't say anything at all.

"Can Jazz still attend practices while she's suspended?" asks Coach Chan.

"According to the league rules, she can be in the gym, but she can't participate until she's been cleared to play." Ms. Calerone turns to Jazz. "That's all for now, Jazz. You should get back to class."

Jazz would rather be anywhere than in the principal's office. She feels as if she's been hit by a truck.

"I can't believe the Hornets are doing this!" yells Coach Chan, once they are out of the office. On court, Coach Chan is a yeller. He yells at the referees. He yells at the players on the court. Sometimes he even yells at players on the bench for something players on the court have done, so Jazz isn't surprised that he's yelling in the school hallway. "Don't worry. That committee is going to see what really happened and you'll be cleared. I'm going to make some calls to the league. See if I can get more details. In the meantime, keep your head up."

Coach Chan storms down the hall and out the door, leaving Jazz alone with her thoughts. *In the heat of the moment, did I mean to hurt Catherine? What if the Fair Play Commission suspends me? Why hasn't Cindy answered any of my calls?*

When she just can't take her thoughts anymore, Jazz runs to a girls' washroom and bursts through the door. In the quiet space, Jazz looks at herself in the mirror. Her thick black eyeliner is running down her face. Jazz hardly recognizes the person staring back at her.

"Stupid," Jazz says to her reflection in the mirror. "You're so stupid!"

As soon as the words leave Jazz's mouth, a strange sensation washes over her. She isn't sure if she feels better or worse, but at least she feels something.

Fifteen minutes later, Jazz wipes mascara from her cheeks. She straightens the front of her shirt and leaves the washroom. Jazz walks to the door of her math class. She slips into her desk just as the bell rings. Before Jazz can say hello to Cindy, Mr. Maxwell strides into class.

"Books away," says Mr. Maxwell. Jazz's eyes widen. "We're having a pop quiz."

The students groan and drop their books on the floor. With the big game last night and the turmoil afterward, Jazz didn't do her homework. She takes out her pencil and writes her name at the top of the paper.

She looks at the questions and her mouth goes dry. The questions might as well be written in Russian. She doesn't even know where to start.

Jazz shakes her head and closes her eyes. She imagines the feeling of grabbing a rebound. She imagines the feeling of jumping, her legs propelling her into the air. She imagines her eyes seeing nothing but the orange basketball. Finally, she imagines reaching out with both hands and pulling the ball toward her body as she lands. Jazz feels a rush of accomplishment.

When Jazz opens her eyes, Mr. Maxwell is collecting the quizzes. The only thing written on Jazz's paper is her name.

4 ON THE SIDELINES

After school, Jazz doesn't know what to do. Usually she'd go to the locker room with the rest of the team to get changed for practice. Since Jazz isn't allowed to practice, she isn't sure if she should change. She isn't sure if the team will want her in the locker room. Finally, Jazz goes to a small washroom near the music room to get changed.

Jazz walks into the gym and sits in the stands.

"What do you think you're doing?" yells Coach Chan.

"Sitting out?"

"This isn't a vacation. Help me get the equipment."

Jazz hops up to help Coach Chan. She rolls out the bin of basketballs while Coach Chan grabs the yellow training cones. The two work in complete silence. When Jazz returns to the gym, the rest of the team is waiting to start practice.

"I can't believe Jazz gave Catherine a concussion," Jazz hears Marie whisper to Cindy. "I wonder if she meant to do it."

"We won't be able to win without her," says Joanne, fiddling with her hands nervously. "She's one of our best players."

"Of course we can still win," says Cindy.

"Yeah," agrees Marie. "Cindy will just have to score more."

"Shouldn't be a problem," says Cindy with a confident smile. "It's my turn to be the star now."

After a deep breath, Jazz steps onto the court. A few of her teammates greet her quietly, but the atmosphere is tense. Jazz moves to stand by Cindy. Cindy looks at Jazz, and Jazz can see that Cindy is coming to a decision.

Finally, Cindy speaks. "What you did last night was gross."

"What?" Could this be her best friend?

"You know what I'm talking about."

"The screen," explains Marie. "Who wants a teammate who plays like *that*?"

"I didn't mean to hurt Catherine."

"Then, why did you elbow her?" asks Cindy. The team goes silent. "I saw you. You elbowed her right in the stomach."

Wait . . . what?

"Did you really elbow Catherine?" asks Janet, one of the forwards.

"No!" says Jazz, but her voice is shaky from the day's emotions. The expressions on her teammates' faces tell Jazz no one is sure who to believe. "It was Catherine who elbowed Joanne before the play started."

"That's true," says Joanne. "She got me right in the ribs."

"Is that why you gave Catherine a concussion?" accuses Marie. "To get her back?"

Jazz remembers thinking that Catherine should pay for elbowing her teammate. "I —"

"What's going on here?" asks Coach Chan as he strides toward the team.

"Nothing," says Cindy quickly.

"Jazz?" asks Coach Chan.

Jazz looks around at her teammates. No one but Ella looks Jazz in the eye. It's as if she's got some terrible disease that the team might catch if they look at her. "Nothing."

"Well, we might as well start with the bad news," begins Coach Chan. "Jazz is suspended for at least a game. She'll attend a hearing tomorrow to determine if she can play for the rest of playoffs."

"If she's allowed to play, are you just going to let her back onto the starting lineup?" asks Cindy.

The team looks at Coach Chan expectantly. "We'll see."

Jazz notices that Marie, the most likely person to replace Jazz on the starting lineup, is smiling like she's won a lifetime supply of candy.

"For now," Coach Chan begins, "we need to get ready for our game against the Grizzlies. I know we beat them by twenty-five points last game, but . . ."

Jazz retreats to the stands. Being so close to the court and not being able to play is the most painful thing she has ever experienced. Every time someone dribbles, the sound echoes in Jazz's ears and she can feel each bounce. She wants nothing more than to feel a basketball against her palm.

The team starts practicing with one of Jazz's favourite rebounding drills. A defensive-rebound drill, it helps players work on getting the ball after the other team has missed a basket. Cindy jumps to grab an easy rebound. But Ella, on the other squad, rushes past Cindy and snatches the ball away for an offensive rebound.

Coach Chan blows his whistle. "Cindy, what have I told you about rebounding?"

"I have to put a body on the person we're defending," Cindy mumbles.

"That's right. You have to be physical. The next person to miss a defensive rebound is going to run sprints."

Coach Chan blows his whistle and the drill continues. Cindy glares at Ella. Ella's cheeks redden slightly and she passes the ball away. Moments later, Joanne takes a jump shot and misses. For the second time, Cindy forgets to put a body on Ella, who runs in to grab the rebound. But at the last moment, Ella pulls her hands away. The ball hits the ground.

Mr. Chan blows his whistle. "Ella, why didn't you catch that ball?" Ella doesn't answer, but Jazz realizes that Ella didn't want to be the reason why Cindy would have to run sprints.

"Not trying your hardest is just as bad as not being physical," says Coach Chan. "You owe me set of sprints."

Cindy smirks. The players clear the court and Coach Chan blows the whistle. Ella runs by herself. A few team members cheer casually, but mostly the players remain quiet while Ella sprints. For the rest of the practice, Jazz sees that Ella stays as far away from Cindy as she can.

When practice is over, the players file out of the gym. Even though Jazz filled their water bottles during practice, they don't look into the stands to say goodbye or to thank her.

Jazz tries to think how she'd react if she thought a teammate had hurt another player on purpose. How is anybody supposed to be friends with someone who gives another girl a concussion? That doesn't just make someone a bad basketball player, it makes them a bad person.

As Jazz puts away the ball bin and the cones in the equipment room, she stares at one of the basketballs longingly. She peeks into the gym. Everyone is gone. The rules say that Jazz isn't allowed to practice with the team, but that doesn't mean she can't practice by herself.

Jazz picks up a basketball and walks onto the court.

At first, she simply spins the ball, passing it back and forth between her hands. Then, she bounces the ball. Instantly, Jazz feels a rush of energy. She starts dribbling on the spot. She bounces the ball behind her back and around her legs. Finally, she looks up at the hoop at the far end of the court.

Jazz begins moving. She walks slowly, dribbling the ball in time with her steps. When she gets to half court, she starts to jog. As she gets closer to the basket, she runs at full speed. She hops off her left foot and extends her right arm toward the basket. For a brief moment, it feels like she is flying. Jazz looks at the corner of the backboard and releases the ball. It falls through the mesh of the basket.

"Nice shot," says a voice from the stands. Jazz turns to see Ella standing in her school clothes. "Don't worry. I'm not going to tell anyone you're taking shots."

"I'm allowed to take shots," says Jazz coldly. It's the same tone Jazz and Cindy always use when they're talking to Ella. But today it doesn't feel right.

Jazz collects the ball and begins taking shots close to the hoop. Ella walks down from the stands and starts rebounding, catching the ball and passing it to Jazz.

"What are you doing?" asks Jazz.

"You've only missed one practice. I'm sure you remember what a rebound is."

"You're teasing me," says Jazz, amazed. Jazz has seen Ella only being serious and careful.

"Maybe," says Ella shyly.

Jazz keeps shooting and Ella keeps rebounding. Other than the ball clanking against the rim of the basket, the gym is quiet. For the first time all day, Jazz feels calm.

"I'd like to make a deal with you," says Ella suddenly.

"What kind of deal?" Jazz asks.

"You know Adam, right? Adam Ross."

"Of course I know Adam," answers Jazz. "He's in three of my classes."

"Well, someone took his watch."

"And?" Jazz takes a step back and continues to shoot. She misses the first few shots and bends her legs to get more power. The next shot goes in, and Jazz smiles when the ball swishes through the net.

"It's a pocket watch. Like the ones you see in movies. It was his grandfather's. And it appears that someone has stolen it."

"What does this have to do with me?"

Ella catches the basketball as it goes through the hoop and holds on to it. She starts tossing it back and forth between her hands. Jazz notices how comfortable Ella looks handling the basketball.

"I think one of your friends stole it."

"What?"

"Specifically, I think Cindy took it."

"Why would she care about Adam's watch?"

"Since when does Cindy need a reason to be

mean?" asks Ella. Her cheeks go red, and she begins bouncing the ball. Still dribbling, she looks up at Jazz. "I don't care why she did it. I'm not interested in getting her in trouble. But Adam really loves that watch. So I want to make a deal with you."

"What kind of deal?"

"You help me get the watch back, and I'll help you with math. *Quid pro quo.*"

"*Quid pro* what?" Jazz says, with a flash of anger. She hates not understanding things.

"It's a Latin expression. It means a favour for a favour."

"Why wouldn't you just say that?" asks Jazz sharply. "And how do you even know I need help with math?"

"I'm in your math class."

"You are?"

"I sit at the back of the class beside Adam."

"Well, I don't think I can help you," answers Jazz. She holds her hands in front of her chest, signalling for Ella to pass her the ball. Ella sends a hard pass to Jazz. "Cindy's not talking to me."

"You don't need to talk to her. I think it might be something you already know."

"You think because I gave Catherine a concussion, I'm a thief too?" spits Jazz.

"No, I think there may be a piece of information that you don't know you know. I have some questions I want to ask you. That's all." Ella moves to leave the court. "If you do that for me, I'll help you with your math homework."

Ella walks into the stands. Jazz keeps shooting, but she is missing more shots than she's making.

When the fifth shot in a row clanks off the rim, Jazz yells, *"Aaaaaaaargh!"*

She collects the ball and realizes Ella is still watching from the top row of the bleachers.

Ella yells down to Jazz. "Just so you know, I saw the whole thing happen. I know you didn't elbow Catherine, and I don't think you meant to give Catherine a concussion."

Jazz squeezes the basketball tightly. "Really?"

"Really," replies Ella simply, and leaves the gym. Jazz is left on the court alone, holding the basketball tightly to her chest.

5 FAIR IS FAIR

Jazz fidgets in her seat in a grey conference room, wearing the dress pants she wore to her great-uncle's funeral two years ago. The pants used to fit perfectly, but Jazz has grown and the pant legs are too short. At first, Jazz thinks that everyone in the room is looking at her because her pants are too short. Then, it dawns on her that everyone is looking at her because they think she's guilty.

The room is filled with coaches, parents, and sports administrators. The adults talk to one another quietly. Jazz sits between Coach Chan and her mother, who are both silent. Suddenly, the door at the back of the room opens, and Catherine and her parents walk in. Away from the court, Catherine could be anyone. Even though she's tall, her grey sweatshirt and slouched shoulders makes her blend in with everyone else in the room. Catherine looks at Jazz. Jazz looks at the floor.

"Won't be long now, Jazz," says Coach Chan. "When they clear you, try not to react."

"Do you really think they'll clear me?"

"They better," says Coach Chan.

Jazz feels her mother's hand touch her knee gently.

A man with a thick moustache walks into the room.

"That's Mr. Vance," says Coach Chan. "He's head of the Fair Play Commission." Behind Mr. Vance, twelve adults walk into the room and sit at the front.

Mr. Vance clears his throat and says, "We are here today to rule on a basketball game between the Ocean View Secondary Hornets and the Fromme Secondary Pipers. In the game, Catherine Hugh suffered an injury as a result of a screen set by Jasmine Smith-Mohapatra. The committee's role is to determine whether Ms. Smith-Mohapatra's screen was fair and, if it was not fair, what the consequences will be."

"Here we go," whispers Coach Chan.

Jazz closes her eyes. She sees the play over and over again in her mind. Every time Jazz remembers setting the screen, the screen gets harder. Jazz can feel Catherine slamming into her chest. Jazz is sure the committee is going to suspend her for the rest of season and for all of next year.

Mr. Vance begins, "After speaking with the referees and reviewing tape from the game, the committee has come to a decision. While the consequence of the screen was severe, the committee has ruled that the screen set by Ms. Smith-Mohapatra was fair. Because of the technical foul assessed by the referee, Jazz Smith-Mohapatra will sit out the first playoff game. However, if the Pipers win that game and continue in playoffs, Ms. Smith-Mohapatra is free to play." Jazz's eyes shoot open. It feels like her chest might burst with relief.

"What about my daughter?" protests Mr. Hugh.

"I'm sure I speak for everyone in the room when I say we hope she has a fast and full recovery," responded Mr. Vance formally.

"She has to sit out the rest of the season while the girl that set that screen gets to play? That isn't fair." Several people in the room nod their heads, and Jazz's eyes start to well with tears. Jazz feels her mom's hand squeeze her knee.

Mr. Vance turns to Catherine's father. "It would be equally unfair to punish someone for a clean screen. We will never know the intent of the screen, but we can be certain Ms. Smith-Mohapatra did not break the rules of the game to set it."

Mr. Vance and the committee get up and leave the room. Jazz sits entirely still. She's flooded with so many emotions, she doesn't know what to do with them. On the one hand, Jazz is relieved. The committee is very official. If they say the screen was fair, then it must have been. On the other hand, Jazz feels that Mr. Hugh is right. Catherine can't play and Jazz can. That seems unfair. Mostly, Jazz feels grateful that in less than a week she'll be back on the basketball court.

"Jazz . . . Jazz!" Jazz realizes her mom's hand is no longer on her leg. Jazz looks up to see her mom standing at the doorway. "It's time to go."

Jazz looks around the room. It is empty. "I never got to say sorry to Catherine."

"You don't have to say sorry," says Coach Chan. His tone is suddenly very chipper. "They cleared you."

"But . . ."

"No *buts*," says Jazz's mom. "It is time to get you back to school."

When Jazz arrives at school, it's lunch and she doesn't know where to go. She wants to go eat lunch with Cindy and tell her the good news, but she doesn't know if Cindy is talking to her. Jazz realizes she's never eaten lunch alone. The last thing Jazz wants is to draw attention to the fact that she's all by herself.

Finally, Jazz decides to go to the gym. Students aren't supposed to be in the gym at lunch, but the equipment room is left open. Jazz sneaks inside.

Alone among the sports balls, cones, and skipping ropes, Jazz eats her sandwich. When she's finished, she goes to the basketball bin and takes out a ball. Jazz takes a deep breath as she spins the ball in her hand. She passes it back and forth between her palms. It feels like a huge weight has been lifted off her shoulders, but Jazz can't forget Mr. Vance's words: "*We will never know the intent . . .*"

The only person who can know what Jazz was thinking before she set the screen is Jazz. But even Jazz isn't sure what she was thinking.

"We shouldn't be down here," says a voice from

outside the equipment room. "There are bound to be consequences if we get caught snooping around the equipment room."

"We won't get caught," replies Ella's voice.

"How do you know she'll be down here?"

"Adam, I know you're better at me in English and physics, but there are certain subjects where I am the expert. Basketball is one of them."

Jazz looks around. Other than locking herself inside a ball bin, there's nowhere to hide.

Suddenly, Ella is at the doorway. She turns to Adam. "I told you so."

Unlike Ella, Adam is very tall, and his legs are so long and thin that he looks like a grasshopper. He wears big, black-rimmed glasses, and his brown hair looks like it hasn't been brushed in years.

"Hello there!" says Adam brightly. "You weren't in English class this morning. Ella informed me about your —" He is stopped by Ella's elbow in his ribs. "Ow! What was that for?"

"How did the hearing go, Jazz?" asks Ella carefully.

"They said the screen was fair," says Jazz. She tries not to smile, but her lips turn to the sky.

"That's great," says Ella.

"It's better than great," adds Adam. "It's downright excellent."

"I still can't play until after the first playoff game."

"That's not ideal," says Adam. "You're arguably the

Pipers' best player. Even against the eighth-place team, it isn't good for the team to be missing their leading scorer and rebounder."

"I'm not the best player," says Jazz. "Do you really keep track of the whole team's statistics in your head?"

"It's more challenging with some players than others, but it keeps me involved in the game." "It's actually pretty neat," says Ella. "We go over all my statistics after every game, so I can keep track of how I'm doing."

"For example," begins Adam. "I keep track of the number of minutes each player plays during a game. In the first ten games of the season, Ella was playing approximately twenty-five minutes per game. But in the last five games, she's been playing close to thirty minutes per game."

"It's been really helpful to me to know this kind of thing," says Ella. "Even though Coach Chan has been yelling at me more, he's also been playing me more. So, I must be doing something right."

Ella holds her hands in front of her chest and Jazz passes her the basketball. The two girls start passing the ball back and forth. Jazz holds her right hand to the side to give Ella a new target. Ella easily passes the ball to Jazz's hand. Adam watches the girls pass the ball, an awestruck and slightly scared expression on his face.

"Do you remember what we talked about yesterday?" Ella asks Jazz.

"About you thinking Cindy stole Adam's watch?"

"Yeah. What do you think about the deal? Does it seem fair to you?"

"I don't know what I think about it," says Jazz. "I don't think Cindy would like it very much."

"Probably not," agrees Adam. Between passes, Ella shoots him a glare.

"She doesn't have to know. You can tell her Coach Chan is making me tutor you in math."

"Because I want Coach Chan to know that I need to be tutored in math," says Jazz sharply. Ella looks away. "I don't betray my friends, Ella."

"You won't have to. I'll just ask you some questions. I can do the rest on my own, and I'll help you with math." Ella stops passing the ball. "Think about it."

Ella and Adam leave. Jazz does nothing but think all through lunch and her afternoon classes. She thinks about the pop quiz she failed. She thinks about Adam's watch. Mostly, she thinks about how the team is going to react to the committee's decision. When practice time finally arrives, Jazz gets to the gym early to get out the cones and fill the water bottles as the team slowly comes into the gym. Coach Chan blows his whistle and everyone circles around him. Jazz holds all the water bottles.

"I have some good news," says Coach Chan. He pats Jazz on the back. "After reviewing the tape, the Fair Play Commission ruled that the screen was fair. Jazz has been cleared to play after Monday."

The team looks at each other. No one says anything.

"Great," says Ella finally. Her voice is barely above a whisper and her cheeks turn bright red, but she keeps talking. "It'll be good to have you back on the court."

"So, she didn't elbow Catherine?" asks Janet.

"Who said anything about elbowing?" asks Coach Chan.

The team looks at Cindy. "I saw her do it. I swear."

"Well, you obviously saw wrong," says Janet.

"That's enough," says Coach Chan. "Jazz will be back and that's what matters. Janet, I want you to lead warm-up."

Janet nods and the team begins to jog around the court.

Cindy snatches her water bottle from Jazz's arms.

"That's where my water bottle went," snarls Cindy. "Give it to me."

"Thanks for filling them," says Ella as she takes hers.

Jazz sits in the stands while the team practices. It's much easier to be on the sidelines now that she knows she'll be able to play again.

"I want us to practice running our plays," says Coach Chan. "Start with *1–4*."

Jazz watches the team run through the play *1–4*. Ella starts with the ball, outside the three-point line that arcs across the court. Ella dribbles the ball while the other players line up in a horizontal line underneath the hoop. She makes a move toward the basket. Jazz knows that if she beats her defender, the other defenders will stay with the offensive players they are defending and let Ella take an open shot, or they will help Ella's defender by stepping in to stop her. If the defence steps in to help, Ella will pass the ball to an open player. Over and over again, Jazz watches as Ella beats her defender. Over and over again, Jazz sees Ella make good decisions about whether to take the shot herself, or to pass the ball to a teammate.

Coach Chan blows his whistle and the team runs to make a circle around him. "We're going to scrimmage for the last ten minutes of practice. I want to watch, so Jazz will referee."

"Can she do that?" asks Joanne tentatively.

"She can't play or practice, but I don't see why she can't referee," answers Coach Chan. He hands Jazz a whistle. Jazz looks at him nervously. She looks around at the team. Ella looks anxious — as if she wants to stop Coach Chan from making Jazz referee — but she stays silent.

The scrimmage begins. Jazz doesn't have very much experience being a referee, but she's played enough to know the rules. She watches the game carefully. Marie gets the ball and makes a move toward the basket, but she moves her feet before she bounces the ball.

Jazz blows the whistle and calls Marie's violation. "Travel."

Marie throws down the ball and Ella rushes over and picks it up. The scrimmage continues. Every time

Marie gets the ball, she moves her feet before she bounces the ball. The first few times Jazz blows the whistle, but the more calls she makes, the more frustrated Marie's team becomes.

"Get it together, girls!" yells Coach Chan.

"I see what you're doing," hisses Cindy suddenly in her ear. "Marie will play your position while you're suspended, and you're trying to make her look bad by calling travels on her."

"I'm not . . . she's . . ." Jazz stutters. Jazz is calling what she sees. At least, she thinks that is what she is doing. Maybe this is like the screen, and Jazz doesn't know what she's really doing.

On the very next play, Marie gets the ball near the sideline. Again, she moves her feet before dribbling. Jazz looks at Coach Chan. He's too busy watching the defender to notice. Jazz doesn't make the call.

After practice, everyone sits in a circle. "Don't forget about my party tomorrow night," Cindy reminds the team. "I expect everyone to be there." Cindy looks at Jazz. "Even you."

6 THE PARTY

Even though it's a cold February night, Jazz has been standing outside Cindy's door for ten minutes. She tucks her hands into her armpits and shivers.

She would never admit it, but it took her more than two hours to get ready for Cindy's party. Beneath Jazz's winter jacket, she's wearing a fitted white T-shirt and her nicest pair of jeans. Her hair is blow-dried and her makeup is perfectly applied. She's ready to celebrate. But now that Jazz is all dressed up, the last thing she wants to do is have fun.

"It won't be that bad." Jazz turns to see Ella, wearing a puffy white winter jacket. She is also wearing a toque, heavy winter gloves, and large snow boots. She looks like she's ready to go snowshoeing to the North Pole. "Well, it might be that bad," Ella admits, "but it won't last very long."

"How do you know how long it'll last?" asks Jazz curiously.

"The girls on the team have the attention span of

goldfish. I usually slip out early."

Jazz tries to remember previous team parties. She doesn't remember Ella leaving early. She barely remembers Ella being at the parties at all. "I just . . . I have a bad feeling."

"About the party?"

"Remember when we almost lost to the Saints?"

"We played particularly poorly," remembers Ella. "It didn't help that the referees were against us."

"Right. Well, before the game, I had this exact same bad feeling." Jazz pauses. She wants to tell Ella that's she's scared the team won't care about the results of the hearing. That everyone will still blame her for what happened to Catherine. She wants to tell Ella that she still blames herself for what happened to Catherine, no matter what the committee said. But Jazz realizes this is the first time she's had a conversation with Ella about anything but basketball.

Ella looks at Cindy's house and then back at Jazz. "Come on."

Jazz and Ella walk to the front door together. When they get there, Ella lifts her hand to knock, but Jazz stops her. "There's a key under the mat. Cindy thinks it's uncool to knock."

Ella shakes her head and mumbles under her breath, "That girl is weirder than a penguin in the Sahara desert."

Despite herself, Jazz laughs. "Did you really just say that?"

The Party

Jazz opens the front door and the girls walk in. Over the years, Jazz has spent hours in Cindy's house, but now she feels like a stranger. Jazz takes off her shoes and places them carefully on the mat in the hall. She hangs her jacket on a hook above them and then leads the way into the living room. Music from a player in the corner plays loudly. Some Pipers' team players sit and talk to one another on the couch. By the fireplace, Cindy and Marie sit with several members of the boys' basketball team.

"I'm going to score twenty points on Monday," announces Cindy.

"It'll be easier now that Jazz isn't playing," adds Marie. "She takes so many shots away from the rest of us."

"Totally," agrees Cindy.

"Hi, Jazz," says Brad. He walks toward her from the kitchen, holding two drinks in his hands.

"Hi," replies Jazz nervously. Ella glances at the two of them and slinks off down the hall.

"Congrats on the hearing today."

"Thanks." Jazz smiles warmly. Maybe people will be able to forget the screen. Maybe she can start to move on.

Before Jazz has time to start a conversation with Brad, she realizes that the room has gone completely silent. Brad notices the attention and looks back at Jazz nervously. He turns and leaves her without saying another word.

Half an hour later, Jazz goes to the kitchen to get a

glass of water. Since she arrived at Cindy's house, not one person has talked to her, although the whole house buzzes with conversations and music. Jazz leans against the wall that separates the kitchen from the living room. One of her favourite songs comes on the stereo and she watches as everyone around her dances.

"Stop it!" Jazz hears a squeal from Cindy and looks to where she is still sitting with Brad.

On the couch, Brad pretends to tickle Cindy. He pulls her onto his lap. Jazz's mouth becomes dry as Brad reaches out his hand and intertwines his fingers with Cindy's. Cindy giggles and Brad smiles nervously. Before Jazz can watch anything else happen, tears fill her eyes. She turns and strides through the kitchen. She pushes her way out onto the back porch.

The cold air is fresh against Jazz's face, drying her tears

Jazz thinks that, if she was smarter, she would've known there would be consequences for her actions. Brad being with Cindy instead of Jazz must be one of those consequences.

"This is all my fault," mutters Jazz. She opens her eyes wide and yells. "I'm so stupid!" Her words disappear into the cold winter air.

Suddenly, Jazz hears a beeping noise behind her. She whirls around. Wearing her white puffy coat and her toque, Ella is curled up on the porch with a cell phone in her hand.

"You're not stupid," says Ella quietly.

"What are you even doing out here?" snaps Jazz. She knows she has no right to be angry, but she can't help but lash out.

Ella's phone beeps again. She looks at the screen and types a quick message. "I'm playing Internet Scrabble with Adam."

"Outside?"

"Outside."

"But it's freezing out here." The more Jazz snaps at Ella, the less she feels like crying. It feels good to be angry.

"Do you know what's worse than a team party?"

"No, what?"

"Having to run sprints while wearing a Halloween costume on a hot summer day." Ella pauses. "That's it. That's the only thing that's worse than a team party."

Jazz has no answer to that. She wipes the tears from her cheeks and looks down at her hands. Black mascara coats her fingers. If she goes back inside, people will know she's been crying.

Jazz starts wiping her cheeks frantically. "How could I be so dumb?"

Suddenly, Ella's hand grabs Jazz's wrist. Ella looks Jazz right in the eye. Her voice is understanding but firm. "Stop it." Ella lets go of Jazz's wrist and backs away. She types something into her phone and then looks up at Jazz. "You aren't stupid."

"Yes, I am!" cries Jazz. "I knew tonight was going to suck! I should never have come. I should never have set that screen. I should —"

"Of course you should've," Ella interrupts.

"What?"

"Of course you should've set the screen."

"How can you say that? I gave Catherine a concussion."

"Catherine got a concussion by accident. The screen was fair. The committee cleared you, and I watched you set the screen. You did everything you were supposed to do. It isn't your fault that Catherine's teammate didn't warn her. It isn't your fault that Catherine bought Joanne's fake. Sometimes people get hurt. That's part of the game."

"Hurting people is part of the game?"

"Accidents are part of the game."

Suddenly, a horn honks from the front of the house. Ella grabs Jazz's wrist again. "Come on."

"Where are we going?"

"Adam's is picking me up. Given that you've been crying, I don't think you want to go back in there."

Jazz nods.

"Good. I texted Adam and told him to make his brother come get us."

"And his brother is doing that?"

"I've been helping Adam's brother with his math homework."

"Aren't you way younger?"

Ella blushes. "I'm taking advanced math before school." Ella pulls Jazz through Cindy's back yard. She opens the fence at the side of the house and walks Jazz to a car parked in front of the house. Adam pops out of the front seat to open the door for them.

"Hello there!" says Adam enthusiastically. He looks at Jazz. "You aren't wearing shoes or a coat. Did they steal your shoes? Sometimes in gym class —"

"She took them off at the front door," interrupts Ella. "I'll go get them."

Ella walks back to Cindy's, leaving Adam and Jazz standing outside the car. Jazz looks away from Adam awkwardly.

"Your makeup seems to have smeared," says Adam, pointing at Jazz's tear-stained cheeks.

"I know," says Jazz through gritted teeth.

Adam's face drops. "I'm sorry. I probably shouldn't have said anything about your makeup. My parents think I talk too much."

"You do talk too much," says Adam's brother from the driver's seat.

Adam ignores him. "The only person who doesn't think I talk too much is Ella. And that's because she's weird. But, you know, weird in a good way." Jazz looks to the door. No sign of Ella. "Actually, you look really nice. Even more so than usual."

"Excuse me?"

"Your outfit. Of course, your clothes are always very stylish, but you look particularly good tonight."

"Thanks, I think."

Ella walks back from Cindy's house and hands Jazz her coat and shoes. "Let's go."

"Finally," says Jazz. Ella and Adam get in the backseat. Jazz sits in the front.

"Thanks for picking us up, Noah," says Ella.

"No problem." Unlike Adam's, Noah's speaking pace is slow and drawn out. "I gotta stop at Robbie's. Any of you in a rush to get home?"

Jazz shakes her head. During the fifteen-minute car ride to Robbie's, Adam babbles aimlessly. At first Jazz thinks he's super annoying but, by the time Noah stops the car, Jazz finds Adam's babbling kind of calming.

Jazz, Adam, and Ella sit in silence as Noah disappears into Robbie's house. Finally, Jazz finds the mirror in the sun shade and starts to gently wipe the mascara stains from her cheeks.

"Thanks, Ella. You know, for tonight and stuff," says Jazz awkwardly. Jazz remembers Cindy and Brad on the couch and makes a decision. "What were the questions you wanted to ask me?"

"Maybe now isn't the best time," says Ella. "I don't want to take advantage of you when you're feeling vulnerable."

"You're the one that said I wasn't betraying my friends," says Jazz defensively. The last thing she needs is pity from Ella. "You want to take that back?"

"No, I don't. You aren't betraying anyone. I've already deduced —"

"Why don't you use normal words?" asks Jazz sharply.

Ella's cheeks redden.

"Because bigger words are more interesting," replies Adam like it's the most obvious thing in the world.

"Have you ever heard anyone else our age using the word 'deduced'?" asks Jazz.

"I bet Sherlock Holmes used 'deduced' when he was our age," argues Adam.

"I've already . . . figured out," begins Ella again, "that if one of your friends did steal the watch, they didn't tell you."

"How do you know?" asks Jazz. "Maybe I'm lying for them."

"You were surprised when I told you about the watch. You've had a . . ." Ella looks up at Jazz. "A *sucky* week. I don't think you'd be a very good liar this week."

"That's smart," says Jazz. "And how do you know Adam didn't lose it?"

"It happened in the middle of English class," explained Adam. "I put the watch in my backpack at the beginning of class. But I drank a big glass of water at lunch, so I had to use the washroom in the middle of English and —"

"I don't need to know about you having to pee," says Jazz.

"Yes, you do. Because it meant I had to go to the washroom," answers Adam. "And when I came back from the washroom, the watch was gone. I never touched my bag."

"So we think someone took it," says Ella.

"People take stuff from me all the time," adds Adam.

"That's terrible," says Jazz honestly. She can't imagine people stealing her stuff every day.

"I'm used to it," says Adam with a shrug. "Usually they return my belongings."

"More specifically, the stolen items magically reappear outside his locker or on top of his gym bag," says Ella. Unlike Adam's, her voice is hard. "But the watch hasn't reappeared."

"Not yet," says Adam hopefully.

"I don't think they know it's important to you," Ella says to Adam.

"So why did they take it?" Jazz asks her.

"For the same reason they steal his shoes. They think it's funny."

"People suck," says Jazz.

"That's not true," says Adam. "Lots of people are wonderful. Like me, for example." Adam pauses to think. He adds, "Ella's pretty great, too."

"So what do you want to ask me?" asks Jazz.

"Last Wednesday at lunch —"

"That was game day," says Jazz tentatively. The last thing she wants to think about is Wednesday.

"Did any of your friends not show up for lunch? Or were any of them late?"

"I, uh, I don't know." Jazz tries to remember Wednesday. She was already nervous about the game. She remembers waiting for Cindy to paint her nails. "Cindy was late for lunch." Jazz's heart sinks. "Brad, too. Oh, and Ashley was late. But I think it's because she was in detention."

"Hmm," says Ella from the backseat. "Were any of them acting strangely during lunch?"

"Not really. Cindy forgot her lunch so we shared mine while she painted my nails."

"Hmm," says Ella again.

"Hmm, what?" demands Jazz. But before Ella can answer, Noah is back in the car with a stack of books. He plops them on Jazz's lap and starts the car up again. The entire ride, Adam rambles about the Pipers' first-round playoff game coming up. The more Adam talks, the more nervous Jazz becomes. She realizes that if the team doesn't win, her season will be over and she won't get to play until next year. Not only that, the gym will be filled with people, and all the people there will have opinions about Jazz's screen.

7 BENCHED

Jazz sits nervously and watches the Pipers warm up. Cindy is extra loud. She squeals and claps every time she scores a basket. The rest of the team feeds off Cindy's energy and playfully drift through the motions. The only player taking warm-up seriously is Ella. Jazz looks at the Grizzlies. They are a small team with no superstar players, but their warm-up routine is serious and disciplined.

Jazz wishes more than anything that she could be on the court instead of sitting on the bench. She reminds herself how lucky she is that she has to sit out only one game. Jazz looks out at the crowd. She sees several people point at the Pipers' bench. It feels as if everyone is pointing at her.

The team finishes warm-up and runs to the bench. Coach Chan announces the starting lineup and gives the pregame talk. "Remember what we practiced this week. We've got to work hard on defence, and everyone needs to focus on getting offensive rebounds."

The team puts their hands together for a cheer. The Pipers' starting lineup walks onto the court. Joanne stands at centre court ready to take the tipoff. She towers over the Grizzlies' player across from her.

The referee throws the ball into the air. Joanne's reaction time is so slow that the much smaller Grizzlies' player is able to win the tipoff. The Grizzlies pass the ball upcourt and score the first two points of the game right away. The Grizzlies' bench cheers loudly. Coach Chan throws his clipboard on the ground.

The Grizzlies defend the Pipers the full length of the court, but Ella is a strong dribbler. She handles the pressure and passes the ball upcourt to Marie. Marie's defender is out of position, and Marie has a clear path to the hoop. She leans toward the basket, and Jazz knows what's going to happen before it does. Marie moves her feet before she bounces the ball.

The referee blows her whistle. "Travel."

Marie looks around, confused. The Grizzlies pass the ball up the court and score an easy basket. Ella gets the ball. She looks at Coach Chan.

"*Up!*" yells Coach Chan, calling the play for her. "*Run Up!*" The players get in their positions. Marie and Cindy are on the same side of the court, with Marie playing in Jazz's usual position. Ella passes the ball to Cindy and runs past Marie. But when Marie goes to screen for Cindy, she doesn't set her feet. The screen isn't strong enough and Cindy's defender easily avoids Marie.

Cindy struggles to keep control of the ball. She throws an ugly shot at the basket and it clanks off the rim. The only player to go for the offensive rebound is Ella.

By the last minute of the first half, the Pipers are losing by ten points. The referee has called six travelling violations on Marie, and *Up* hasn't worked once. Coach Chan's face is so red from yelling that it looks like his head might explode. In the locker room between the halves, the players look at each other accusingly.

"The referee sucks," says Marie. "She keeps calling me on travels."

"That's because you're travelling every time you touch the ball," snaps Coach Chan.

"Why didn't you tell me in practice?" yells Marie. Ashley puts her hand on Marie's back to try to calm her.

"Where is our rebounding?" asks Coach Chan. But he clearly doesn't really want an answer. "Ella, why isn't *Up* working?"

"It isn't working because she's passing me the ball too late," accuses Cindy. "I'm not getting open. That must be why."

Ella clenches her jaw and looks at the floor.

"What do you think, Ella?" demands Coach Chan.

Ella's cheeks redden. "I'll try to pass Cindy the ball earlier."

"You'd better," sneers Cindy.

When the horn sounds to signal the end of half time, the Pipers run back to the court. Ella stops to fill her water bottle at the sink. Jazz stays behind.

"What do you really think?" Jazz asks Ella.

Ella runs her hands through her hair and looks over her shoulder. "I think you're a better player than both Marie and Cindy. So when you set the screen in *Up*, both defenders are worried about you. That's why Cindy always gets open so easily with Marie setting the screen." Ella pauses. "I think if we want to win we have to stop running *Up*."

Joanne opens the locker room door. "Come on, Ella!"

Ella takes a deep breath and Jazz can see how desperately Ella wants to win. She also sees how scared Ella is of Coach Chan and Cindy.

People steal things from Adam. Jazz wonders if the same thing happens to Ella. Following Ella as she runs out the door and back onto the court, Jazz looks up into the stands. Adam sits there, holding a sign with Ella's number on it. He waves at Jazz.

Jazz beckons to Adam and he hustles down the stairs.

"It's a very close game," says Adam. "The Grizzlies are leading in every statistical category." Adam takes a breath, and it looks as if he's going to start a long colour commentary about the game so far.

Jazz cuts Adam off. "How do you get Ella to stand up for herself?"

"It's a challenge. If she doesn't have time to think,

she can react intuitively and stand her ground. But she's always thinking."

Jazz nods and walks back to the Pipers' bench.

The Pipers have the ball for the first play of the game.

"Try *Up!*" yells Coach Chan.

Ella nods. Joanne passes the ball to Ella. Ella calls *Up*. Everyone runs to their positions. Before the defence is set, Ella passes Cindy the ball. The pass is hard and fast, and it comes very close to hitting Cindy in the face. For what feels like the hundredth time, Marie's screen is weak. Cindy's defender easily blocks Cindy as she dribbles toward the basket. In a panic, Cindy passes the ball to Ella. Cindy's pass is really a high throw, and tiny Ella has to jump to catch the ball. Ella fakes at the basket. Her defender jumps, and Ella dribbles past her to the basket to score two easy points. Ella's basket cuts the Grizzlies lead to eight points.

Jazz watches the game unfold. Every offensive play, one of the Pipers makes a mistake. Every time, Ella manages to get open to help her teammates. Jazz watches as Ella beats her defender over and over again. Unlike Cindy, who always makes a scene when she scores, Ella quietly runs back on defence after a basket. By the three-quarter break, the score is tied.

"We're still getting beat on the rebounds, but that's better," says Coach Chan at the bench. "Keep running *Up*. It's bound to work eventually."

Benched

Ella looks at the ground. Jazz looks at the score. She really wants her team to win this game.

"Coach," says Jazz tentatively. "I think maybe we should try running *1–4*."

Ella and Cindy both stare at Jazz, with open-mouthed surprise.

"But that's the play where Ella drives from the top," whines Cindy. "No one else touches the ball."

"That's not true," says Coach Chan. "If other defenders move to defend Ella, she'll pass the ball to open players. It's worth a try. Run it once and see how it goes."

Ella nods. The quarter begins. After a good defensive play, Joanne finally manages to get a rebound. She passes the ball to Ella. Ella looks nervously at the bench.

"*1–4*," Coach Chan tells her.

Ella calls the play and the players run to their positions. Ella stays outside the three-point line while the other players line up underneath the hoop. When everyone is in place, Ella makes a hard move to the right. When her defender lunges after her, Ella crosses the ball in front of her and drives to the basket. None of the Grizzlies' players step in to help Ella's defender. Ella scores a basket. For the first time all game, the Pipers take the lead and the crowd cheers loudly. Jazz looks into the stands. Adam is jumping up and down on the spot.

On defence, the Pipers play hard. The Grizzlies shoot the ball and miss. Marie gets the rebound. Ella rushes to Marie and grabs the ball.

"Again!" yells Coach Chan to Ella. "Run *1–4* again."

This time, Ella doesn't think twice. She calls the play.

The Grizzlies' coach calls to his team, "Help. Everyone has to help!"

Again, Ella easily beats her defender, but this time several Grizzlies step in front of her. Ella passes the ball to Joanne, who is wide open under the basket. Joanne scores.

Jazz watches as Ella starts to command the court. She no longer looks to Coach Chan to call the plays. Instead, she dribbles up the court and calls the play on her own. Ella beats her defender again and again, always making the right decision to shoot or to pass to the open player.

In the last eight minutes of the game, the Pipers score fifteen points and the Grizzles score only four. When the final buzzer sounds, the Pipers have won the game by ten points.

"Great game!" cheers Coach Chan. "Who knew you had it in you, Ella?"

As the team heads to the locker room, Jazz tugs on Ella's wrist. "You knew you could do that. You were just too scared to say anything."

"I didn't know," says Ella quietly. "Not for sure."

"Well, now you do."

"And now you get to play," says Ella with a smile.

8 BACK TO NORMAL?

"Well?" asks Jazz nervously. Ella stares at Jazz's math notebook, checking her work. "I got the answer wrong, didn't I?"

"No," says Ella. "You got it right. And your work is right, too."

"Really? I thought for sure I'd gotten that one wrong."

"Why?"

"I get confused by brackets sometimes," admits Jazz. "Cindy was supposed to be helping me, but most of the time I ended up copying her homework. She said it was easier that way."

"That's not actually very helpful."

"I guess not." Jazz looks at Winston, the stuffed moose, sitting by her pillow. She gets up and grabs him.

"Nice moose," says Ella playfully.

"Usually I keep him under the bed. But I've kind of needed him this week," explains Jazz. She looks down at Winston. "Cindy gave him to me when we were kids.

I don't understand her. She's never been mean to me before. Not like this."

"Must have been nice to be on Cindy's good side for so long," says Ella bitterly. Then she takes a deep breath. "I mean, I'm sorry she's not talking to you these days."

"Do you know why she isn't?" asks Jazz carefully.

"Cindy doesn't need a reason to be mean," replies Ella. "But if I had to guess, I'd say it's because she wants the chance to be the star of the team."

"Really?"

"She's always talking about you two winning the MVP award together. Maybe she doesn't want to share."

Jazz thinks about Adam and all the statistics he keeps in his head. "She wouldn't win it anyway, would she?"

"What do you mean?"

"Cindy's not one of the best players on the team. There's Joanne and you."

"What about me?"

"You were great in yesterday's game."

"I was okay."

"You were great," says Jazz. "And I think Cindy knows it. Maybe that's why she picks on you all the time."

Jazz hears a car drive up and park in the driveway. A few moments later, the front door opens.

"Jazz, I'm home!" announces Jazz's mom.

"We're in my room!" yells Jazz. Jazz's mom appears at the door to Jazz's room. She looks surprised to see Ella there. "Mom, this is Ella. She's on my basketball team."

"Nice to meet you, Ella. Would you like to stay for dinner?"

"No, thank you. I'm just helping Jazz with her homework."

"That's really nice of you."

"Thanks," says Ella. "But I should get going. Dad wants me home for dinner."

After Ella leaves, Jazz's mom looks at Jazz with a curious expression on her face. "Doesn't Cindy usually help you with your homework?"

"Cindy's not talking to me right now," says Jazz.

"Do you want to talk about it?"

"Not really." Jazz realizes she does want to talk about it, but not with her mother.

"Okay. But if you change your mind, I'm here to listen." When Jazz doesn't reply, she goes on. "Ella seems nice."

"She is."

"Maybe it's a good thing you're making new friends."

"Maybe."

"How are you feeling about practice tomorrow?"

"You remembered!" Jazz exclaims, surprised.

"Your dad and I are going to try to remember more often." Jazz's mom sighs. "When I was at your hearing, I realized I don't know much about you and your basketball team. I'd like to change that. We can't make it to your next game, but if you advance to the championship finals, we'll be there. Now, what do you want for dinner?"

"Pizza?"

"You need your vegetables."

"Veggie pizza?"

"Maybe," says Jazz's mom with a smile as she leaves Jazz's room.

Jazz spots Winston on her bed. He's lying beside her math book, with his nose between the pages as if he's trying to learn about brackets. Jazz remembers that Cindy wrapped him herself. It had taken Jazz three minutes to rip through the layers of tape and paper. When she saw a moose, her favourite animal, Jazz smiled so wide her cheeks hurt. Cindy and Jazz spent the afternoon thinking of just the right name for the moose. Now, Jazz wonders if the memory of giving her Winston would make Cindy smile, or if she would think it was childish and uncool.

Sitting down beside Winston, Jazz thinks about Cindy and Ella. Cindy's never been nice to Ella, but Jazz hadn't realized just how mean Cindy is to her. She's never thought about how Cindy might make Ella feel. What else hasn't she noticed about Cindy?

"Jazz!" yells Jazz's mom. "Can you come help set the table for dinner, please?"

"Just a second."

Jazz picks up Winston for a moment. Then she reaches down to stuff him back under the bed.

Back to Normal?

★★★

Jazz stops outside the locker room. Even though it's only a practice, she is nervous. It's the first time she's dressed for practice since the game against the Hornets.

"Hi," says Cindy, as she falls into step with Jazz. They walk into the locker room together. "Where were you at lunch today?"

Jazz wants to ask Cindy why she suddenly cares, but she doesn't want to talk to Cindy in front of their teammates.

"In the gym," Jazz decides to just answer. "I wanted to touch a ball before practice today."

"I'm glad you're practicing," says Joanne from the corner of the room. "We're gonna need you for the game against the Beavers tomorrow."

Jazz notices other team members nodding in agreement.

"It's true," Cindy says in a small voice. "We need you if we're going to win."

When Jazz gets on the court, she takes a deep breath, but it doesn't help. Being on the basketball court feels strange. Jazz grabs a ball and starts taking shots. Every time the ball goes through the net, Jazz's shoulders tense up. Something doesn't feel right.

Coach Chan blows his whistle. "First off, I'd like to welcome Jazz back to practice." The team claps loudly. "The Beavers are a tough semi-final match-up for us. They are bigger and stronger than the Grizzlies. We need to be ready to fight for every rebound. That should be easier with our best rebounder back on the court." Coach Chan looks at Jazz and smiles.

They start practice with Jazz's favourite rebounding drill. The first time through the drill, Ella passes Jazz the ball and Jazz catches it easily. Joanne, the defender, doesn't move to challenge her. Jazz shoots. The ball clanks off the side of the rim. Normally Jazz would run full speed to try to get the rebound, but she suddenly realizes that she doesn't want to accidentally bump into Joanne. Joanne jumps and grabs the rebound.

"Come on, Jazz!" says Coach Chan. "Where's your killer instinct?"

The word "killer" echoes in Jazz's mind. As the drill continues, Jazz runs through the motions. Except for one instance, where a rebound falls directly in her hands, Jazz doesn't get any rebounds.

Halfway through practice, Coach Chan talks about one-on-one moves. "The more our offensive players can beat their defenders one-on-one, the stronger our team will be. Ella, you did a great job in the game last night. Take the ball at the top of the three-point line and show everyone the move you used last night. Cindy, try to defend her."

"No problem," says Cindy.

Ella reluctantly takes the ball. The team stands at half court and watches. Moving at half speed, Ella dribbles the ball to her right.

"Start again, Ella. Full speed," says Coach Chan.

"Scared you won't be able to beat me?" Cindy taunts.

Ella returns to her starting position. She takes two hard dribbles to her right. Thinking that Ella is going to change directions, like she did in the game, Cindy doesn't defend the move. Ella blows passed Cindy and scores a basket.

"Good work," says Coach Chan. "Did everyone see Ella's speed?"

"She cheated," whines Cindy. "She didn't do the move."

"She didn't do the move because she didn't have to," replies Coach Chan. "It's a good lesson for all of us. Take what the defender gives you. Ella, do it again."

Ella takes the ball outside the three-point line again. Cindy stands ready to defend. Ella takes two hard dribbles to the right. Cindy's expression is determined as she lunges for the ball. Ella easily bounces the ball away from Cindy and dribbles toward the basket. Ella scores again.

"Nice work, Ella!" says Coach Chan. "Everyone pair up. I want you to play one-on-one. Remember — take what the defender gives you! Jazz and Joanne, you're our tallest players, so I want you paired."

Jazz and Joanne go to a basket. Joanne is a painfully slow defender, and Jazz scores easily. Out of the corner of her eye, Jazz watches Ella and Cindy. Ella easily beats

Cindy over and over. Each time, Cindy's defensive play becomes more aggressive.

"Once you've both had a turn on offence, play a game," calls Coach Chan. "The first person to score three baskets wins."

As Jazz and Joanne play one-on-one, Jazz easily beats Joanne 3–0.

"Coach Chan, we're done," announces Joanne.

"Grab some water and wait for everyone else to finish," he says approvingly.

Drinking from a water bottle she didn't have to fill, Jazz watches Cindy and Ella. Cindy dribbles to her right. She's bigger than Ella and, for a moment, it looks like she is going to run over her. At the last moment, Ella reaches out her hand and steals the ball from Cindy. Instead of taking the ball to the basket, Ella hands it back to Cindy.

"You think you're so good?" sneers Cindy. "You're no one. You've got no friends."

Jazz notices that Cindy waited until Coach Chan was helping Marie at the other end of the court and couldn't hear her. Jazz and Joanne exchange uncomfortable looks.

Cindy dribbles to the right, bouncing the ball in front of her body, where it's easy for a defender to steal. Ella reaches out her hand but, at the last second, she pulls back. As Cindy dribbles toward the basket, Ella doesn't even pretend to defend her. Cindy scores and smiles brightly. Jazz cringes as she watches the same thing happen twice more. Each time, Ella goes at half speed and lets Cindy beat her. Each time, Cindy's confidence grows.

Coach Chan blows his whistle. "Good practice, team! I want everyone to rest up tonight. Tomorrow's a big game."

The team moves to the locker room, but Ella stays behind.

"Hey, Jazz!" says Cindy. "Can you hang out tonight? It feels like I haven't talked to you in forever."

Jazz wonders if Cindy has lost her memory. "I can't. I promised Mom I'd be home for dinner."

"Okay. Well, give me a call after. I have so much stuff to tell you."

Jazz grits her teeth. How can Cindy pretend that everything is normal? Before she can follow Cindy to ask her, Coach Chan calls her over.

"Good first practice back, Jazz," he says. "You were a little tentative. Stay tough. Don't let the suspension affect your game. Make sure you're ready for tomorrow."

Without waiting for Jazz's answer, Coach Chan leaves the gym.

But Jazz finds she is not alone in the gym. At the far end of the court, Ella is practicing her passing by throwing the basketball against a wall. Again and again, the ball pounds against the wall.

"Hello there," says Adam, suddenly standing beside her. "How was practice?"

"Where did you come from?" asks Jazz, smiling.

"I was attending a chess club meeting."

"We have a chess club?"

"We do. We are the second-best chess club in our district. I'm the president. How was practice?"

"Practice wasn't that much fun."

"Why?"

"Something didn't feel right."

"Perhaps you're nervous?" offers Adam. "The Pipers have never made it to the finals before. If you win, you'll be the first team in school history to play in a championship game."

"I know," says Jazz flatly. "I'm going to go talk to Ella."

"I'll come with you," says Adam. He takes off his shoes and Jazz shoots him a questioning look. "Ella says I can't wear my boots on the basketball court," he explains,

As they approach Ella, they see tears streaming down her face.

"I don't want to talk to you," says Ella quietly. Jazz's heart sinks. "Either of you."

"What happened?" asks Adam with a worried look on his face.

Ella doesn't answer.

"Adam, let me talk to her for a minute," says Jazz.

Adam nods and returns to the stands. Jazz watches as Ella keeps passing the ball to the wall. Finally, Jazz intercepts the ball as it bounces.

"Give it back," says Ella.

"I saw what happened with Cindy," says Jazz.

"Great."

"Why did you let her beat you like that?"

"You heard what she said."

"About not having friends?" When Ella doesn't reply, Jazz shrugs. "She was just trying to get back at you because you're so much better than she is. It shouldn't bug you. It's not like it's true. You've got Adam."

"Adam doesn't count."

"How does Adam not count? He seems like a really good friend."

"Great, I have one friend."

"What about me?"

"Aren't you and Cindy friends again?"

"Um . . . I don't know. She was being really nice to me today, but we haven't talked yet."

Jazz passes the ball back to Ella. Ella starts practicing dribbling, easily bouncing the ball around and between her legs.

"Actually," Jazz says slowly, "everyone was being really nice to me today. I don't get it."

Ella shakes her head. "Seriously? You have no idea why they were being nice to you again?"

"Because of the decision from the hearing, I guess?"

Ella takes the ball and throws it like a baseball against the wall.

"If you don't know, then you really are stupid," says Ella. The words hit Jazz hard and tears prick the back of her eyes. "The team is being nice to you because they realized we can't win the championship without you."

With that, Ella passes the ball hard at Jazz's chest and storms out the gym. Jazz is left in the middle of the court holding the basketball, alone.

9 ONE ON ONE

Jazz stands outside the lunchroom, looking through the glass doors. She watches Cindy, Brad, Marie, and the rest of the team eating lunch. Cindy says something and everyone laughs. As Jazz enters the lunchroom, Cindy looks up and sees her.

"You didn't call last night," Cindy says.

"I was doing my math homework." Jazz mutters.

"Do you want me to help you?"

"Someone else is helping me." Jazz wonders if Ella is right about why Cindy wants to be friends again. She decides to find out. "Can we go somewhere quiet, so we can talk? Just you and me?"

"I'm eating lunch," says Cindy. "We can talk later."

"We need to talk now," says Jazz.

Cindy leans closer and drops her voice. "Don't be mad about the elbowing thing. That really is what I saw."

"What you *thought* you saw," corrects Jazz. She doesn't want to have this conversation in the middle of the cafeteria.

"Whatever. I'm sorry, all right?" Cindy grabs Jazz's wrist and pulls her toward the table. Jazz sits down at the table across from Brad.

Brad smiles brightly. "Excited for the game tonight?"

"Nervous," Jazz replies honestly.

"Me, too," adds Marie. She drops her voice to a whisper. "I've never played in a semi-final game before."

"It'll be like every other game," says Cindy reassuringly. "Only there will be way more people there to watch."

"I'm going to come watch," says Brad. "It'll be my second game this season."

"Isn't he awesome?" says Cindy proudly.

Jazz thinks about Adam, who has attended every one of the Pipers' games. She thinks about how Cindy is acting as if they've been talking all week. Jazz balls her hands into fists under the table, trying to hold in the anger she feels bubbling inside.

"I'm glad you'll be back for tonight's game," says Marie.

"Totally," adds Cindy. "Now that you can play, we'll win for sure."

Jazz's stomach tightens into a knot. Ella was right. Marie and Cindy are being nice to Jazz only because they want to win. Jazz squeezes her fists tighter.

"I don't feel good," says Jazz.

"You're not getting sick are you?" asks Cindy.

"No, I think I'm nervous. I'm going to sit in the gym."

"You're so dedicated," says Marie.

The gym is quiet and empty. It gives Jazz the space to think. For the first time since the game against the Hornets, Jazz doesn't feel sad or helpless. She feels angry. She's angry at Coach Chan for telling her to set a hard screen. She's angry at herself for hurting Catherine. Most of all, she's angry at Cindy and the rest of her teammates. Ella was right. They don't really care about Jazz. They only care that she has been cleared to play because they think they won't win without her.

Instead of crying, Jazz lets out a long, low yell. The sound of her voice echoes around the empty gym. Then Jazz reaches into her backpack and pulls out a grey hooded sweatshirt. She'd been thinking of wearing a sweatshirt to school all week, but she didn't want to give Cindy another reason not to talk to her.

Jazz pulls the sweatshirt over her head and leaves the gym.

★★★

Jazz stands in front of the mirror. On top of her bag is the plastic wrap from her cream cheese and cucumber sandwich. She has three yellow hair elastics around her wrist. As always, Jazz runs her fingers through her hair ten times, then flips her head back and uses three yellow hair elastics to tie her hair in a ponytail. Usually, Jazz finds the beat of her pregame music calming, but today it's making her frantic. She takes out the ear buds just as Ella walks into the locker room.

"You're late, Ella," says Cindy pointedly.

Ella's cheeks turn bright red and she looks at the floor.

"Cindy, leave her alone," says Jazz.

"What? She *is* late," replies Cindy. Jazz feels Cindy's eyes on her, but doesn't look up. She keeps staring in the mirror.

The tension breaks as Coach Chan walks into the locker room. "Let's get ready to play, ladies! The Beavers are a good team. I want everyone ready to warm up in ten minutes."

From the way the ball feels against the pads of her fingers, to the way the court feels against the soles of her shoes, Jazz is fully aware of every sensation during warm-up. Her mind is moving at the speed of light. Jazz can't stop it. She can't even slow it down.

Jazz looks over her shoulder at the Beavers. Coach Chan was right. They are bigger and stronger than the Grizzlies. She tells herself over and over that the team needs her to be aggressive. They need her to play her best game.

When warm-up ends, Jazz is sweating and her hands are shaking. She stands in the circle around Coach Chan. "Their best player is Number 9, Carly Veers. She is a good shooter. Ella, I want you to defend her. Stick to her like glue."

"Okay," replies Ella nervously.

The team puts their hands together for a cheer. Coach Chan pulls Jazz aside as the rest of the team heads onto the court. "You know you might get some extra attention from the crowd because it's your first game back. Do your best to ignore them."

Jazz looks into the crowd. All the eyes staring at the court feel cold and judgmental. Suddenly, Jazz sees Adam sitting in his usual spot. He is holding a sign that reads: "*Go, Ella #10!*" When Adam sees that Jazz has spotted him, he stands up. Taller than the people around him, he blocks their view and they start calling him to sit down. Adam doesn't notice. He flips the sign, and on the other side of the green poster paper, it reads: "*Welcome back, Jazz #12!*" Adam grins at her.

Jazz walks onto the court and lines up at centre. She is defending the Beavers' Number 13. Her eyes on the referees off the court, Number 13 stands beside Jazz and uses her hip to push Jazz to the side. Usually Jazz would push back, but she decides it's easier to move out of the way.

The referee blows the whistle and throws the ball to start the game. Joanne loses the tipoff, which is tapped in Number 13's direction. Jazz's first instinct is to step forward and grab the ball. But she'd have to push Number 13 out of the way to get to there first. Jazz lets Number 13 get the ball.

"Nice try, Jazz," yells Coach Chan. "You'll get the next one."

Number 13 passes the ball to Number 9, Carly Veers. Carly's expression is determined and focused. She fakes, but Ella doesn't buy it. Carly takes a hard dribble to the basket, but Ella is fast enough to keep Carly in front of her. Eventually, Carly is forced to pass the ball to one of her teammates. Jazz can tell from Carly's face that she isn't used to having to deal with a defender as good as Ella.

The Beavers' Number 13 gets the ball. She puts her shoulder down and dribbles at Jazz. Unable to react quickly enough, Number 13 runs into Jazz and bounces the ball off Jazz's foot. The ball goes out of bounds and the referee blows the whistle. Since Jazz was the last person to touch the ball before it went out of bounds, the referee signals for the Beavers to take the ball. "

Number 13 turns to her bench and yells, "Coach, she pushed me!"

The gym goes silent.

The Beavers' coach yells, "You've got to watch that Number 12, ref!"

The referee doesn't respond, and the crowd boos. Jazz realizes they're booing because they think she should've been called for a foul.

Number 13 pushes passed Jazz. Rattled by the last play, Jazz allows her to get a good position under the basket. The ball flies through the air toward Number 13. Jazz knows that if she gets the ball that close to the basket, she's going to score.

But Ella sees Jazz hesitating, and darts away from Carly. She catches the ball and starts running down the court. With a head start, Ella scores an easy basket. The Pipers are the first team to score. The crowd cheers.

The next time down the court, Number 13 sprints to her position under the basket where she's most likely to score a basket. Jazz attempts to stand her ground and puts her hand on Number 13's hip for leverage.

"Get your hands off me" hisses Number 13 the moment Jazz touches her. "*So* dirty."

"I'm not …" Jazz looks at her hand on Number 13's hip. Is Jazz pushing Number 13 or is she playing good defence? Before Jazz can decide, Carly gets the ball on the wing and shoots. Ella plays good defence and Carly misses the shot. Jazz turns to get the defensive rebound, but several players rush toward the ball. Not wanting to run into anyone, Jazz steps away. Number 13 gets the rebound and scores.

"Come on, Jazz! Rebound," yells Coach Chan from the sidelines.

Jazz runs down the court on defence. Ella calls the play *Up*, and Jazz heads to her spot at the top of the key. Number 13 stays close to Jazz, keeping one hand firmly on Jazz's hip. Ella passes the ball to Cindy. Jazz waits for Ella to pass her and then moves to set the screen for Cindy. Jazz plants her feet, ready to be hit hard in the chest. But at the last moment, Jazz hesitates and softens her shoulder.

Unable to beat her defender without a perfect screen, Cindy bobbles the ball and throws it in Ella's direction. Ella jumps to catch the ball. Forced to shoot off balance, Cindy misses the throw, and the Beavers get the ball.

"Subbing you," calls Marie from the scorekeeper's table. Almost relieved, Jazz runs off the court.

At the bench, Coach Chan stops Jazz from sitting down. "What's going on out there? You're not being physical. It's like you don't want the ball."

"I don't know," says Jazz frantically. "I don't know what's happening."

As the game goes on, every time Marie touches the ball, she travels, so Coach Chan is forced to put Jazz back in the game. But Jazz is still off her game. She sets terrible screens and she can't get a rebound.

When the horn sounds for the end of the first half, Jazz is starting to think it might be better if she went and sat in the stands for the second half.

The Pipers sit in the locker room and wait for Coach Chan.

"You should run *1–4*," says Marie to Ella. "That worked last game."

"Carly is way too fast. Ella can't beat her," says Cindy. "Keep running *Up*. It'll work."

"I think our effort is there. Some of our players aren't having their strongest games," says Coach Chan looking right at Jazz. "And we've missed some easy shots. But I'm confident we'll be better in the second half. Keep working hard, Pipers!"

The team claps, then everyone puts their hands together for a cheer.

As the rest of the team leaves the locker room, Jazz stays behind. When she's sure everyone is gone, she yells, "AAAAARGH!"

She grabs her water bottle and throws it against the wall. It doesn't make her feel any better, but it does spray water all over the locker-room wall. Jazz runs to the court to join her team.

Halfway through the third quarter, Jazz is still playing terribly. The worse she plays, the more frustrated she feels. The more frustrated she feels, the less she trusts herself.

Number 13 gets the ball in the key. Jazz is tentative on defence. When Number 13 shoots, Jazz slaps accidentally slaps her wrist. The referee calls a foul.

Coach Chan calls Jazz over to the bench. "Jazz, we need you out there. Whatever is going through your head, stop it."

Jazz nods and returns to the court. Number 13 scores both her free throws. Then the Pipers get the ball. Ella calls *Up*, but Cindy's defender won't let her get open. Ella can't pass Cindy the ball. Jazz runs to the sideline to fill Cindy's spot.

"Play my position," Jazz says to Cindy.

"But I don't know what to do," says Cindy.

"Wait for Ella to run past you. Then set a screen for me." says Jazz. She feels silly telling Cindy what to do where the other team can hear, but she doesn't have a choice.

Ella passes Jazz the ball, then runs past Cindy toward the basket. Ella ends up wide open near the hoop. With Cindy tying up Jazz's defence, Jazz makes a difficult pass to Ella, who scores a basket.

The next time down the court on offence, Ella immediately passes the ball to Jazz at the top of the key. She ignores the confused expressions on Cindy and Ashley's faces and makes a move toward the basket to receive Jazz's pass. Again, Ella scores. The third time down the court on offence, Ella passes the ball to Jazz again, but this time, Ella can't get open right away. Jazz turns to face the basket and takes a few dribbles to the side. She passes the ball to Ella, who gets fouled and earns two free throws.

Jazz decides that she's going to focus on one thing. She'll help Ella score by passing her the ball. It won't make playing any more fun, but it sure beats feeling useless.

In the last minute of the fourth quarter, the Beavers are down by one point. Carly gets the ball near the sideline. She makes a strong fake and beats Ella, leaving Jazz her next defender. Usually Jazz would step in front of Carly to try to stop her, but Jazz simply holds her arms in the air and stands still. Carly scores and the Beavers go up a point.

Coach Chan calls a timeout. The Pipers run to the bench.

"The timeout means we're going to get the ball on the sideline." Coach Chan hesitates for a moment. "I want us to run *Chop.*"

"What?" cry Jazz and Ella in unison. Ella's cheeks go bright red.

"You heard me," says Coach Chan. "It's one of our best plays. This is a semi-final game. I expect you to play your roles."

As the team heads back to the court, Jazz turns to Coach Chan and whispers, "Please, sub me out. I can't set that screen. "

"Of course you can," says Coach Chan. "You've set it a thousand times. You can do this."

Jazz gulps. She slowly walks onto the court, feeling the colour drain from her cheeks. Everyone in the gym is watching her. It's as if they know that Coach Chan has called *Chop* — and that she will have to set a hard screen and maybe hurt someone.

Suddenly, Ella sprints toward Jazz. She whispers, "I want you to come to the ball. I'm going to pass it to you. Pass it right back."

"What?"

"Come to the ball," Ella says again. "As soon as I slap it."

Ella hustles to stand by the referee. When the referee holds out the ball, Ella grabs it and slaps it. Joanne makes her usual fake, but Jazz doesn't move to set the screen. Instead, she runs toward the sideline. Ella passes the ball to Jazz and runs onto the court, holding out her hands. Jazz passes the ball to Ella. Carly sees that Ella is about to shoot and grabs Ella's wrist. Ella shoots, but the ball doesn't go anywhere near the net.

The referee blows the whistle. "Foul! Pipers' Number 10 will shoot two free throws."

Neither team has any timeouts left. The players line up for Ella's free throws with only three seconds left in the game. Jazz's heart is beating in her throat. She knows that if Ella misses either of her shots, the Pipers will lose. If they lose the game, she tells herself, it will be her own fault for being too scared to play her role and help the team.

The referee passes Ella the ball. She bounces it five times and then spins it so it rests perfectly in her palm. Jazz holds her breath. Ella releases the ball. Jazz watches it float through the air. It feels like the world has slowed down and a breeze could knock the ball off course. Finally, the basketball reaches the rim. It clanks against the front of the rim.

Jazz's heart sinks.

Then, suddenly, the ball rolls and falls through the net. The score is tied.

Joanne gives Ella an enthusiastic high-five. Jazz is still too nervous to move. The referee passes Ella the ball. She bounces it five times and spins it so it rests perfectly in her palm. This time, Ella's hands are steady, and everything moves in normal time. Ella shoots and scores.

After the free throw, the Pipers play good defence for the three seconds left in the game. The horn sounds, and the Pipers win by one point!

Jazz stands and watches her team celebrate. She should feel excited, but the only thing she feels is relief. Relief that Ella made the shots. Relief that no one got hurt. Relief that the game is over.

Coach Chan gives his after-game speech right on the court as the gym starts to empty. He tells them they have a day off before the next practice. As the team leaves the gym, Coach Chan calls Ella to the side. Jazz can't hear what he says to Ella, but his gestures are firm.

As Coach Chan strides away from Ella, she walks to the bench with tears in her eyes.

"What happened?" asked Jazz.

"He yelled at me for not running the play, but I couldn't run it. It wasn't fair to ask you to set the screen." Ella plops down on the bench and starts to sob. "And I shouldn't have called you stupid yesterday. I'm sorry."

"You were right."

"You're not stupid."

"No, about the Cindy. She's only being nice to me because she wants us to win. But I can't help with that. *Aaaaargh!*"

Adam runs on the court, sliding across the floor in his socks. "*You're* yelling, and *you're* crying. How is that possible? Ella, you scored your free throws and now the Pipers are going to the championship finals. You're a hero."

"I'm no one's hero," says Ella.

"You're my hero," says Adam seriously.

Ella cries even harder as she gets up and leaves the gym.

Adam turns to Jazz. "But you won the game. Isn't that what's it's about?"

"I don't know what it's about anymore," replies Jazz with a shrug. All she knows is that basketball isn't as fun as it used to be.

10 ADAM'S PLAN

Jazz leans against a wall outside the lunchroom and stares at a poster advertising the Pipers' championship game against the Hornets on Monday. Trying to ignore the students who congratulate her on making it to the final, Jazz peeks through the doors.

At a long table in the middle of the lunchroom, Cindy and Marie smile brightly and welcome the attention. They are dressed in matching jeans and short pink T-shirts. Jazz looks down at her grey hooded sweatshirt and loose jeans. She's glad that she's not dressed like Cindy anymore. After a deep breath, Jazz turns her back on the lunchroom and walks through the crowded school to the gym.

At the gym door, Jazz finds Adam and Ella. Ella's posture is firm, and she is frowning. The moment Adam sees Jazz, he waves for her to join them.

"Hello there, Jazz!" says Adam.

"What's going on?" asks Jazz.

"Adam won't let me in the gym," says Ella.

"Correction," says Adam. "I'm not letting either of you enter the gymnasium."

"Like you can stop us," says Jazz, trying to walk by Adam.

Adam steps forward, towering over them.

"What are you going to do to stop us from going in?" says Ella defiantly.

"While the door is always open, students are not supposed to be in the gymnasium at lunch," Adam says. He is suddenly very interested in a rock under his shoe. "I've thought about it, and I'm willing to inform a teacher that you are breaking the rules."

"You'd tell on us?" asks Jazz.

"You wouldn't!" says Ella.

"I think this is important, so I would," says Adam. "I have something to say, but you have to promise not to interrupt."

As much as Jazz would like Ella to stand up for herself, she doesn't think yelling at Adam outside the gym is a good idea.

"We'll listen," says Jazz quickly.

"We will?" asks Ella.

"Lunch lasts fifty minutes," explains Jazz. "He'll have to stop talking when the bell rings."

"I can always keep going after school," Adam points out. He grabs Ella and Jazz and tugs them away from the gym to the library. He drops their hands and leads them between two rows of books.

"What are we doing here?" asks Jazz.

"We needed somewhere quiet," replies Adam. "The library is a quiet place, particularly during lunch hour. We're going to talk about our feelings."

"I thought boys didn't like talking about their feelings," says Jazz, her arms crossed over her chest.

"We aren't going to talk about my feelings. We're going to talk about yours."

Ella rolls her eyes.

"What kind of feelings?" asks Jazz.

"I want you to answer one easy question," says Adam seriously. "I would like both of you to promise to tell the truth."

"Okay," says Jazz tentatively.

"Fine," replies Ella.

"Do you think basketball is fun?"

"Usually," answers Jazz.

"Not usually," says Adam. "Right this second. How does basketball make you feel? Is it fun?"

Jazz thinks about the game last night. Every play was frustrating. She couldn't get a rebound. She played terrible defence. Worst of all, Jazz felt the whole night like she couldn't trust herself.

"No," says Jazz. "It's not fun."

"Ella?" asks Adam gently.

Ella's forehead is scrunched like she's trying to solve a mystery. "No," she says. Her voice is small and quiet.

"Excellent," says Adam.

"How is that excellent?" asks Jazz.

"It's a good first step. I couldn't stop thinking about your game last night. You'd just won the biggest game of your lives, and both of you were really upset. As I understand it, basketball is a game, and games are supposed to be fun. If you aren't having fun, that's a really big problem."

There is a long silence. Jazz waits for Adam to start rambling about the game or the team's statistics, but he doesn't say anything. Instead, he looks at Ella, waiting for her to respond. His expression is so caring, Jazz feels like she is intruding.

Ella looks up at Adam. "Look, Adam, I get that you're trying to help. But there's only a week left until the championship game. There's nothing we can do to fix this now." Ella moves to get up. "I'm going to go to the gym to practice."

"No, you're not." Adam grabs Ella by the hand. His ears turn bright red, but his voice is firm. "You get to play in a championship game. Not everyone gets to do that."

"It's a grade nine championship," says Ella. She pulls her hand away from Adam. "It's not that big a deal."

"You know what the chances of me playing in a championship basketball game are? None. Zip. Zero. Zilch."

"That's because you can't catch," says Ella with a small smile.

"That's correct. I don't have very strong hand-eye coordination, but that's okay. I excel in other areas. But you, you're good at basketball and you've trained hard all year. You deserve to have fun." Adam turns to Jazz. "So do you. The whole team does."

"I don't know what the team deserves," mumbles Jazz.

"You both want to win. How can you win if you aren't having any fun? "

"I'm sure we can manage it," says Ella dryly.

"What if I told you I think we can make it fun again?"

Jazz is curious. "How?"

"I have a plan," says Adam. "But you have to trust me."

"Adam, why are you even helping me?" asks Jazz.

"Why wouldn't I help you?"

"You and I aren't . . . weren't . . . Are we friends?"

"We can be if you want to be," says Adam with a wide smile.

Jazz doesn't say anything, but she nods. Adam's smile gets impossibly wider.

"All right," says Jazz finally. "I'll go along with your plan. Ella?"

"Fine, I'm in, too," sighs Ella. "What's first?"

"Remember," Adam says, "you promised to trust me."

"This isn't good," mutters Ella.

"Coach Chan gave you the night off," continues Adam. "You don't have practice until tomorrow night. I'm ordering you not to touch or talk about basketball until tomorrow at practice."

"No," says Jazz instantly.

"Not a chance," adds Ella.

Adam holds up his hand, "You've both said basketball isn't fun right now, so why would you want to play? Give me a good reason why you should do something that isn't fun."

"It feels weird not to," says Jazz honestly.

Ella agrees. "I feel like I should at least touch a ball."

"Those are not good reasons," says Adam.

"So what are we supposed to do instead?" asks Jazz.

"I don't know," answers Adam. "You can come with me. I have chess club after school."

"That is so nerdy," says Jazz before she can stop herself.

"Still want to be my friend?" Adam asks with a smile.

"Yeah," says Jazz.

"Jazz, I could help you with math again," offers Ella. "Sure."

"Fantastic," says Adam. The lunch bell rings and Adam hops to his feet. As he strides out of the library, he looks over his shoulder. "Remember, no basketball."

As the two girls leave the library, Jazz asks, "Did you ever figure out who stole Adam's watch?"

"I've got a guess," says Ella coldly.

"Who was it?"

Ella turns her head and looks at Jazz. "Like I said all along. It was Cindy."

11 MYSTERY SOLVED

The next afternoon, Jazz gets to practice early. As promised, she hasn't touched a basketball since the game against the Beavers. Even though it's only been 47 hours and 23 minutes, it feels like it's been years. She realizes it's the first time she's been excited about basketball since the first game against the Hornets.

"We made it," says Jazz when Ella walks into the gym. "A whole day without basketball."

"Let's see if it helps," says Ella.

Cindy walks in and looks at Ella, who instantly backs away. Jazz wants to grab Ella and pull her forward.

"So, what are you two talking about?" asks Cindy accusingly. "And where were you at lunch today?"

Before Jazz can answer, Coach Chan walks in. "I hope you all had time to celebrate the win against the Beavers. That was a big game, and I'm very proud of all of you. But the celebration ends now. We need to get ready for the championship game against the Hornets next week. As you all know, Catherine Hugh won't be playing. But the rest of the team has come together and is playing great basketball. We'll have to play our best game if we want to beat them."

The team spends the first part of practice working on dribbling. Jazz enjoys challenging herself with difficult behind-the-back and through-the-legs moves.

After the second water break, Coach Chan sets up a rebounding drill. "We're going to practice defensive rebounding. I want one offensive line and one defensive line. I will throw the ball off the backboard, and both the offensive player and the defensive players will try to get the rebound. If the defensive player doesn't get the rebound, she will stay on defence. If the defensive player does get the rebound, she will go to the back of the offensive line."

The team gets into two lines, and Jazz rushes to be the first defender. Coach Chan throws the ball off the backboard. The ball bounces into Jazz's hands. She catches it easily and hands it to Coach Chan, then runs to the back of the line.

Coach Chan throws the ball off the backboard again. This time, Ella is defending Cindy. Ella grabs the rebound, but Cindy bumps Ella with her hip, causing Ella to drop the ball.

"Come on, Ella. Hold it with two hands," says Coach Chan.

Ella is forced to play defence again.

The closer Jazz gets to the front of the line, the

more nervous she becomes. When she reaches the front of the offensive line, Marie is defending her. Coach Chan throws the ball against the backboard. Jazz's first instinct is to lower her shoulder and push by Marie to get the ball. But she freezes. Marie grabs an easy rebound.

"That wasn't a good enough effort, Jazz," says Coach Chan. "Ten push-ups. Now."

Jazz does her push-ups and goes to the back of the line. When she gets to the front, she again tries to force herself to go for the rebound. But the moment Coach Chan throws the ball off the backboard, Jazz freezes.

"Ten more push-ups, Jazz," says Coach Chan roughly.

By the end of practice, Jazz has spent more time doing push-ups than practicing. Her arms are sore, her jaw is clenched, and she can't wait until she can leave the gym.

Finally, Coach Chan blows the whistle. "Practice is over. Good work today, Pipers!"

The team slowly leaves the gym, but Jazz stays behind. She picks up a basketball and kicks it to the ceiling.

"I am so stupid!" yells Jazz as she thinks about the rebounding drill. When the basketball hits the ground, Jazz raises her foot and kicks it again. "Stupid!"

"No, you're not!" Jazz looks up. Adam is standing at the top of the bleachers, staring at her. Embarrassed, Jazz looks at her feet. Adam runs down the steps, takes off his shoes, and joins Jazz on the court. "Don't say that about yourself."

"Sorry," says Jazz sheepishly. "I was just frustrated."

"My plan didn't work?" asks Adam with slumped shoulders.

"It did," answers Jazz. Adam's face lights up. "I was having fun at the start of practice. But then we did this rebounding drill, and I was terrible."

"Hmm." Adam looks around the gym. "Where's Ella?"

"In the locker room?" Jazz suggests.

"That's strange. She specifically instructed me to meet her here after your practice."

"I'll go look for her," says Jazz.

Jazz walks to the locker room. As she walks down the hallway, she hears Cindy's voice echoing off the walls. "If you tell anyone about this, I'm going to make sure Adam and everyone else knows what a loser you are. Then, you won't have any friends at all." Jazz starts running. "I can ruin your life. Do you understa —"

Jazz bursts through the door. Cindy and Ella are standing nose-to-nose in the middle of the locker room. Cindy has her index finger pointed at Ella's face and Ella has tears streaming down her cheeks. They both turn to look at Jazz.

"What's happening here?" Jazz asks, looking at Ella.

"Nothing," sneers Cindy. "Right, Ella?"

Ella doesn't say anything. She looks at Jazz through

narrowed eyes, like she knows how Jazz is going to react. Jazz has to make a choice and she has to make it now.

"Something is happening," insists Jazz.

"I just said it's nothing," replies Cindy.

"I heard you," replies Jazz with a little more confidence, "and I'm not blind. Why is Ella crying?"

"Because she's a freak."

"Or maybe because you said you'd make it so no one will be her friend anymore."

Cindy's face drops.

"I heard you in the hallway," Jazz continues. "So I'm going to ask you again. What's happening?"

There is a long silence.

"She stole Adam's watch," says Ella finally. Ella looks down. Jazz follows her gaze. There is a gold pocket watch sitting on top of Cindy's backpack.

Jazz feels as if an elastic band has snapped inside her. All the anger and confusion of the last few weeks bubbles up in her chest.

"Why would you do that?" Jazz's voice is so shrill and loud that both Cindy and Ella take a step backward.

"It's just *Adam*," says Cindy dismissively.

Jazz flaps her arms and stomps her foot three times. "Who do you think you are? Since when do you steal people's things? Since when do you tell people you're going to ruin their lives? Since when do you not stand by me?"

"What are you —"

"I'm not done talking yet!" yells Jazz. Cindy's eyes go wide. "After the game against the Hornets, you turned on me. You didn't stand up for me. You didn't even talk to me for a week. I was confused and angry and . . ." Jazz takes a deep breath to try to collect herself. "I needed you. But you were too busy flirting with Brad and stealing people's watches to notice. And now you're threatening one of my friends. Who do you think you are?"

"Since when is Ella your friend?" asks Cindy.

"Since now," says Jazz. Grabbing Adam's watch, she turns her back on Cindy. "Come on, Ella. Let's go."

Stunned, Ella's simply nods and follows Jazz out the locker-room door. When they get to the gym, they find Adam awkwardly throwing a basketball with two hands. The ball clanks against the rim.

"This is fun," says Adam. "I see why you both enjoy it so much." He throws the ball at the basket again and runs after it when he misses. "I feel like a golden retriever chasing a tennis ball. I could do this for hours."

Adam's expression changes when he sees Ella. Her eyes are puffy and her nose is red from crying. "What happened?"

Ella doesn't say anything. Jazz realizes she doesn't want to tell Adam what Cindy said to her.

"We found your watch," says Jazz quickly.

Adam's face fills with emotions that Jazz can't place. So she hands the watch to Adam.

"Where did you find it?" he asks.

"Cindy stole it."

Adam bites his lip. "I was trying to get over it, but I thought this watch was gone forever. Thanks, Jazz."

"Thank Ella. She's the one who figured it out."

Adam looks at Ella. Her face is still frozen in an awe. She looks at Jazz. "You stood up for me."

"Of course I did," says Jazz. "She was yelling at you."

"No one's ever stood up for me before," says Ella.

"Well," says Adam, "there's a first time for everything." He pauses and he turns to Jazz. "Wait. Does that mean you yelled at Cindy?"

"Yeah," says Jazz. "I didn't mean to. I just . . . I've been really mad at her, and there hasn't been a good time to talk to her. I can't believe she'd steal your watch. Why would she do that?"

"I think she was going to give it to Brad," says Ella carefully.

"Oh," says Jazz. Her heart sinks. "I don't know what's happening to her. She wasn't always so . . . awful."

Ella looks as if she wants to disagree, but Adam shoots her a stern look.

"Well, it was good that you expressed your feelings," says Adam. "That reminds me. How are you two feeling? How was practice? Jazz, you said the beginning went well. What about you, Ella?"

"I felt okay until we did this rebounding drill," says Ella.

"Me, too," says Jazz.

"It must have been the worst rebounding drill ever," says Adam.

"I couldn't get a rebound," says Jazz.

"That's not exactly true," says Ella. "You were fine on defence, but you wouldn't move on offence." Ella turns to Adam. "Coach Chan kept making her do push-ups because he thought she wasn't trying hard enough. But that wasn't the problem." She turns to Jazz. "I think you couldn't get past being afraid to hurt someone."

Adam crinkles his eyebrows together in concentration. Suddenly, he looks up. "I have an idea. I want you both to stay after practice tomorrow. I am determined to make basketball fun again."

12 PLAN B

Jazz runs up and down the court. It is the last practice before the championship game, and Jazz's emotions are everywhere. One minute, she is excited about the big game. The next minute, she's scared to be on the court. It's as if there's a whole butterfly *war* going on in her stomach.

Sweat drips down Jazz's face as she catches the ball on offence. She makes a hard pass to Ella, who catches the ball and scores an easy two-point shot.

Coach Chan blows the whistle. "Good pass, Jazz, but don't be scared to take it to the hoop yourself."

Jazz nods. She wonders if Coach Chan has even noticed that she has entirely stopped trying to score or rebound. Instead, she's been running up and down the court, trying to get herself in positions where she doesn't have to be physical. At least this way, Jazz isn't constantly worried that she's going to hurt someone. And it turns out that Jazz is a pretty good passer.

"For the last five minutes of practice, we're going to

play a game," announces Coach Chan. "I want everyone defending someone they don't usually practice against."

Jazz's team is on defence. She looks around. Everyone has switched defenders and the only player for Jazz to defend is Cindy. Jazz takes a deep breath and goes to stand in front of Cindy. They don't say anything. They don't even look at each other.

"Let's get started!" yells Coach Chan. He blows the whistle. Jazz follows Cindy around the court. Just as Cindy is about to get the ball, Jazz anticipates the pass and sticks out her hand. The basketball hits her palm and Jazz controls it, bouncing it on the ground as she runs toward the basket. Jazz can hear Cindy's footsteps chasing her.

"I'm with you!" yells Ella.

At the last moment, Jazz passes the ball to Ella, who scores. Cindy runs into Jazz, tackling her to the ground.

Coach Chan blows the whistle. "Cindy! What was that for?"

"I thought Jazz was going to shoot. It was an accident."

"You okay, Jazz?"

"Fine," says Jazz, but she whispers to Cindy, "You did that on purpose."

"I didn't," says Cindy between breaths. "But I should've. You stole the ball from me."

The game continues. A few plays later, Jazz is on offence and gets the ball near the basket. Normally she'd make a strong move and try to score, but this time hangs back and shoots from a safe distance. The ball goes wide of its target.

Coach Chan blows the whistle. "Come on, Jazz. Be more aggressive!"

"Sorry, Coach," sighs Jazz, frustrated with herself.

"Everyone, come in!" says Coach Chan. "Monday is a big game. Probably the biggest game most of you have ever played. Get lots of rest this weekend so that we're ready for Monday."

Suddenly, someone grabs Jazz's wrist.

"Meet me in the hall by the equipment room in five minutes," says Cindy. "We need to talk."

She strides off toward the change room.

"Everything okay, Jazz?" asks Ella.

"I don't know."

"Adam wanted us to meet him here after practice," Ella reminds her.

"I know. I'll be back."

Jazz collects her bag and water bottle and goes to the hall. Two minutes later, Cindy arrives. She has already changed out of her practice clothes and back into her jeans. The two girls stare at each other for a minute.

"You wanted to talk?" says Jazz finally.

"You yelled at me yesterday," replies Cindy.

"You stole Adam's watch. Were you really going to give it to Brad?"

"So what if I was?" replies Cindy. "It isn't fair. You're

already one of the team's best players. You can't have the perfect boyfriend, too."

"What does having a boyfriend have to do with being a good basketball player?"

"You wouldn't understand."

"Try me."

"Everyone wants to be the star — "

"Everyone?" challenges Jazz. "Or you?"

Cindy scowls. "I used to be one of the stars, but now you get to take the important shots and win all the awards. Do you have any idea how much that sucks for me?"

"I don't know if you've noticed, but I've had the worst month. Catherine got hurt. I was suspended from basketball. My best friend accused me of playing dirty. All my teammates turned on me . . . Wait . . . you did it on purpose didn't you?"

"What are you talking about?"

Jazz shakes her head. She can't believe it took her so long to put the pieces together. "You told everyone I elbowed Catherine so they'd turn on me and you'd get the chance to be the team leader." When Cindy doesn't reply, Jazz presses. "Didn't you?"

"What if I did?"

"You lied to me when you apologized in the cafeteria. We've been friends since we were six. Does that not matter to you at all?!"

Cindy's expression softens a tiny bit.

"I don't like not being the best," says Cindy, her tone matter-of-fact instead of angry. "That's why I wanted to give Brad the watch. I wanted to win something."

"I don't think a boyfriend is something you can win."

"You know what I mean."

"Not really."

"I wanted to beat you, and I can't beat you on the basketball court," Cindy admits. "I wanted Brad to choose me."

"That's ridiculous."

"Maybe it is," Cindy concedes, "but I can't be friends with you if you're going to be better than me. I can't handle it."

"That's . . ." *Selfish* and *immature* are the first two words that come to mind, but Jazz knows saying them aloud will turn their argument into a screaming match. Jazz looks at Cindy, with her tight-fitting jeans and her defiant stare. It's hard to believe Cindy is the same girl who once gave Jazz a stuffed moose as a present. Jazz wonders if she's changed as much as Cindy has.

What do you say to a friend who can't be happy for your successes? The moment the question crosses her mind, Jazz knows the answer. "If you can't handle supporting me when I win, then I can't be friends with you either."

A long silence hangs between the girls as the full meaning of their words sinks in.

Cindy is the first to state the obvious conclusion.

"Then, maybe we're not friends anymore."

"Maybe not."

Finally, Cindy turns and leaves. Standing alone in the hall, Jazz feels like crying, but no tears come. As strange as it feels to lose Cindy, it would feel even stranger to stay friends with someone who cared more about being the best than about their friendship. Jazz takes a deep breath and walks back to the court to join Ella.

"How'd it go with Cindy?" asks Ella.

"I don't think we're friends anymore."

"I'm sorry."

"No, you're not. You don't like Cindy."

Ella takes a deep breath, and forces a smile. "Who knows? Maybe she'll change for the better one day."

"Do you really believe that?"

There's a long silence.

"No," Ella answers finally, with a laugh, "but it was the right thing to say. Besides, at the start of this year, I wouldn't have thought you and I would be friends either. So you never know."

"I guess." Jazz looks up into the stands. "What the heck is that?"

At the top of the stands, there is a large figure. It is wearing a strange combination of hockey and football gear, complete with a white hockey-goalie's mask. The figure takes off the mask.

"Hello there!" says Adam waving. He lumbers down the steps and stumbles onto the court.

"What are you doing?" asks Jazz.

"We're going to make basketball fun again," says Adam.

"And you wearing *that* is going to help how?"

"We're going to play one-on-one."

"No," says Jazz nervously. "I don't want to."

"Sometimes it is important to do things you do not want to do."

"It won't even work," says Jazz. "No offence, but I've seen you play basketball, and you aren't very good."

"Aha!" says Adam. "I thought of that. So we'll play two-on-one." He starts pulling out more hockey gear from a duffle bag at the side of the court. "My brother said I could borrow his gear. I'm wearing his old stuff, and Ella's going to wear his new stuff. Great, right?"

"I've smelled your brother's hockey gear," says Ella. "I'm not wearing it."

"Yes, you are."

Jazz sees that Adam has the same look he wore when he went on and on about statistics.

After a five-minute argument, Ella slips into the hockey gear. "How am I going to play like this?"

"Do your best," says Adam. "We'll both defend Jazz." Adam hands Jazz the ball. Jazz takes a deep breath. She tentatively takes a dribble to the right, moving so slowly that Ella steals the ball, even burdened with her hockey gear.

"Try again," says Adam.

"I don't want to," says Jazz. "This isn't any fun."

"It isn't any fun because you're scared of hurting us. But you don't have anything to be scared of. Look." Adam walks up to Ella and pushes her to the ground.

"What was that for?" demands Ella.

Adam leans over to help her up. "To prove my point. You're fine, aren't you?"

Ella stands. "Yeah, I'm fine." She stands up and shoves Adam. He falls to the ground, but the hockey gear protects him and he bounces back up right away.

"See! Try again, Jazz." Adam hands Jazz the ball again. This time Jazz shot fakes. Ella doesn't defend the fake, so Jazz follows it with a shot. The ball soars toward the rim. Jazz gently nudges Adam and manages to come up with an awkward offensive rebound.

"Good start," says Adam.

"I feel stupid," says Jazz.

"You should try being me," grumbles Ella from under her hockey mask.

Jazz takes the ball again. Encouraged that Adam wasn't injured by the nudge, Jazz does another shot fake. This time Ella lunges, so Jazz puts her shoulder down and pushes past her to the basket to score.

For an hour, Jazz plays against Ella and Adam. Long before the end of the hour, everyone is sweating. Jazz doesn't think twice when she jumps over Ella to get a rebound.

"Good job," says Adam.

"Better," says Jazz. "But in the game on Monday, the Hornets won't be wearing hockey gear."

"They don't need to be," says Adam. "What were you thinking while we've been playing?"

"Nothing, really."

"Exactly! You were just you. When you play on Monday, don't think. Just be you. We'll keep doing this all weekend. You can get an abundance of practice being you."

13 A NEW START

Jazz stands in front of the locker-room mirror with three yellow hair elastics around her wrist. She runs her hands through her hair ten times and flips back her head to catch her hair in her ponytail. With her hair done perfectly and her jersey hanging off her shoulders, Jazz is ready to play. She closes her eyes and listens to her music. She wants to win this game. She wants to play better than she did in the game against the Beavers. Can she get over her hesitation and play her regular aggressive game?

Coach Chan's pregame talk is short and to the point. "This is it. What we've worked for all season. The Hornets are a good team, and we're a good team. But I think if we work hard and stay disciplined, we can be the better team today."

The team puts their hands together and cheers. "Go, Pipers!"

All through warm-up, Jazz can feel Catherine Hugh's eyes watching her from the bench. Jazz takes a shot and Catherine watches. Jazz passes the ball and Catherine watches. Jazz accidentally bumps into a teammate and Catherine smiles like she knows a terrible truth about Jazz. Finally, Jazz can't stand being watched anymore. She puts down the basketball and walks over to where Catherine is sitting. Jazz can feel everyone in the stands watching.

"Hi," says Jazz when she's close enough. Catherine doesn't say anything. "I just wanted to say that I'm sorry you got hurt."

"But you aren't sorry for setting the screen?" asks Catherine coldly.

Jazz takes a deep breath. She looks over her shoulder. Coach Chan yells, "Jazz, what you are doing?"

"No," says Jazz, turning back to Catherine. "I'm not sorry for setting the screen. It was a fair play, and I never meant for anyone to get hurt." Catherine crosses her arms defiantly across her chest. "But, I'm sorry you did."

Jazz returns to the court to continue warming up. She suddenly feels lighter, now that she's said something. As the team runs to the bench after warm-up, Jazz looks into the stands. She sees her mom sitting in the corner. In the front row, Adam holds a sign that reads: "*Win or Lose, Pipers are #1!*"

Jazz gets ready for the tipoff.

"Oh, look," says the Hornets' Number 14 as Jazz takes her position. "It's the dirtiest player in the league."

Jazz closes her eyes. Even though they shouldn't, the words hurt.

"You better keep your hands off me," hisses Number 14 to Jazz.

"Ref," calls Ella suddenly. "Can you watch Number 14? She's harassing my teammate."

"Yeah, right!" Number 14 snaps at Ella.

For an instant, Ella's cheeks turn bright red and she looks like she wants to curl up and hide. But then she raises her chin, looking Number 14 square in the eye. "You don't get to talk to my friend like that."

"That's enough, girls," says the referee. He tosses the ball in the air.

Joanne wins the tipoff and tips it to Jazz. Jazz grabs the ball, but Number 14 rips it from Jazz's hands. For a moment, Jazz's stomach does a flip. Then she lets instinct take over. She puts both hands on the ball and grabs it back, surprising Number 14 with her strength. Jazz throws the ball upcourt to Ashley, who scores.

The Hornets pass the ball back down the court. Jazz is the first player on defence. She faces two Hornets' players charging the basket at full speed.

In her head, Jazz repeats, "Be yourself. Be yourself. Be yourself."

Jazz sees one of the Hornets put her shoulder down. A step ahead, Jazz sets her feet on the ground and squares her shoulders to the player. The player hits Jazz in the chest as she jumps to score a basket. Both Jazz and the Hornets' player hit the ground hard. The gym goes silent as both girls roll onto their sides.

Jazz hears the Hornets' coach yell, "Number 12's a danger, ref! Get her off the court."

Jazz looks up at the referee. The referee puts the whistle in his mouth and blows it. "Offensive foul, Hornets' Number 9!"

Ella runs over to help Jazz up. "Good play, Jazz."

Jazz looks into the stands. The audience is split. The Pipers' fans cheer loudly while the Hornets' fans boo the referee's call.

The game continues, and Ella dribbles the ball up court. She calls the play: *"Up!"*

Jazz goes to her spot and jostles with Number 14 for position. The Hornets' defence is tight, and Ella has to work hard to pass the ball to Cindy. Jazz waits for Ella to pass her, and takes a few steps toward Cindy. Number 14 is so busy pushing Jazz, she forgets to tell her teammate that the screen is coming. Jazz sets her feet on the ground and crosses her arms over her chest. Cindy's defender slams into Jazz's chest and hits the ground. Cindy uses the screen to score a basket.

The Hornets' coach throws his clipboard and starts screaming at the referee. "Did you see that? I told you, she's a dirty player!" The coach turns to Jazz. "I see what you're doing. You shouldn't be on the court."

The referee blows his whistle and Jazz's heart sinks. But she sees the referee walk to the Hornets' coach and put his hand into a *T*, signalling a technical foul on the coach for arguing with the referee. The Hornets' coach goes silent. The referee says sternly, "You can't verbally attack players. Do you understand me?"

The coach nods. Jazz clenches her fists. This isn't the way she wanted the game to start. In her head, she chants, "Be yourself. Be yourself."

Through every play in the first quarter, Jazz continues to repeat those words to herself. She misses a few rebounds, and Number 14 scores a couple of easy baskets. But Jazz isn't playing terribly. When Jazz pictured herself playing in a championship game, she never thought that not playing terribly would be the best she could hope for.

At halftime, the score is tied.

Coach Chan walks into the locker room. He turns to Ella. "All right, Ella. What's working out there? What's not?"

"*Up* is working," answers Cindy.

Jazz looks at Ella. She's staring at the ground.

"Okay," says Coach Chan. "Let's keep running that and —"

"No," Jazz says, interrupting the coach.

"What?" asks Coach Chan.

"Ella doesn't want to run *Up*," replies Jazz. She looks at Ella and gives her a second chance to speak up. "Right?"

"*Up* is working half the time," says Ella hesitantly. "We need to run other plays, too. I can beat my defender off the dribble. We should run *1–4*."

"We should?" asks Coach Chan.

"Yeah," says Ella, a bit more confidently.

"Ella's the point guard," says Joanne. "It's her job to call the plays."

Ella looks up, amazed that two people have stood up for her. Jazz smiles brightly and looks at the team. Everyone nods.

The Pipers' players run onto the court for the second half. Jazz looks into the stands and sees that every seat is full. When she sees Adam with his giant sign and his face painted in the green and yellow school colour, she smiles. As in their first game against the Hornets, the crowd is buzzing with excitement.

The whole season comes down to the next twenty minutes, thinks Jazz. Her desire to win strengthens with each second.

The Pipers start the half with the basketball.

"*1–4*," yells Ella and her teammates set up for the play.

"No," says Cindy. "Run *Up*." A couple of the girls change to their spots for *Up*.

Ella bounces the ball between her legs. She looks at Jazz and then at Cindy. Protecting the ball from her defender by dribbling behind her back, Ella calls more forcefully, "No! Run *1–4*."

Everyone but Cindy runs to her spot for *1–4*. Ella looks at Cindy as if to pass her the ball. But at the last moment, Ella shifts her weight. Ella beats her defender, so Jazz's defender steps in to help. Ella passes the ball, and Jazz scores.

From the bench, Coach Chan yells, "Cindy! Run the play or sit on the bench!"

Next time down the court, Ella runs *1–4* again. This time, it is Cindy's defender who leaves her mark to help protect the basket. Ella passes the ball to Cindy, who is wide open for a shot. Cindy shoots, but the ball clanks off the rim.

Before she has time to think, Jazz is running to grab the offensive rebound. She and Number 14 jump into the air at the same time. Jazz can sense they're going to collide, so she pulls back and lets Number 14 get the rebound.

Off balance, Jazz falls to the ground. By the time she gets on her feet, the ball is already down the court. The Hornets score an easy two-point basket.

Throughout the third quarter, with the score tied, Ella alternates between running *Up* and *1–4*. The Hornets' Number 14 goes out of her way to elbow Jazz on every offensive play and Jazz can feel a bruise forming on her hip. With thirty seconds left in the third quarter, Number 14 gets the ball. She puts her shoulder down and runs into Jazz's chest, knocking her to the ground.

The referee blows the whistle. "Foul on the Pipers', Number 12.

Jazz sighs. The Hornets all high-five Number 14 as she walks to the free-throw line.

The Hornets' point guard looks at Jazz. "Keep playing hard," she says to her teammate. "She can't stop you."

Number 14 looks at Jazz and smirks. Jazz realizes that the Hornets suspect Jazz is scared of being physical, and they are using it against her. The referee hands Number 14 the ball. She shoots and scores her free throw.

The third quarter ends with the Pipers down by two points. In the huddle, Coach Chan says, "One quarter left, guys!"

"Girls," says Ella. "We're *girls*."

"Right. Girls. The game is starting to get physical. We need to match their intensity."

Jazz's heartbeat pounds in her chest. If Number 14 gets any more physical, Jazz won't be able to stop her from scoring.

"Jazz!" yells a voice in the stands. "Jazz!!" Jazz looks for the voice. She sees Adam jumping up and down. The people sitting around him look away, embarrassed.

Adam flips his sign. It reads: "*Don't forget to have fun!*"

"I wish it was that easy," says Jazz under her breath.

"Maybe it can be," says Ella smiling at Adam jumping in the stands. "You had fun when we played on the weekend, right?"

"Yeah," sighs Jazz as they walk onto the court. "But that's because you were wearing hockey gear, and no one was watching. I didn't have anything to prove."

"So pretend no one's watching. Pretend your defender is wearing hockey gear."

"But she's not," says Jazz.

"Try pretending she is and see what happens." Ella walks to her spot on the court. "Because I don't know about you, but I really *really* want to win this game."

Jazz nods. The game is fast and physical, just as Coach Chan said. But the Pipers manage to tie up the game.

Number 14 beats Jazz down the court and gets good position. Jazz tries to imagine that she's wearing hockey gear. Instead of backing away from the contact, Jazz slowly applies pressure to Number 14's hip. Inch by inch, Jazz pushes Number 14 out of position. When the Hornets' player looks to pass Number 14 the ball, she is no longer open, and the shot goes just wide of its mark. The rebound lands in Jazz's hand. Jazz passes the ball to Ella and they run up the court.

"*Up!*" yells Ella.

There are seven minutes left in the quarter. Number 14 puts her forearm on Jazz's hip and starts to push Jazz out of position. Jazz sets her feet and refuses to be moved. Number 14 pushes harder, leaning heavily on Jazz's hip. Jazz stands her ground. Ella passes the ball to Cindy and, when Jazz darts away to set the screen, Number 14 tips and loses her balance.

Seeing that Number 14 isn't defending Jazz, Cindy passes Jazz the ball. Jazz catches it and scores a basket.

The Pipers lead by two points.

On every possession, Jazz tests the limits of her strength. By the last minute of the quarter, Jazz no longer needs to pretend Number 14 is wearing hockey gear.

With less than a minute left in the game, the Pipers still lead by one point. The Hornets have the ball at centre court. The Hornets' coach calls a play and all the Hornets get in position. Three passes into the play, Number 14 gets the ball at the top of the key. She bounces the ball to drive and Jazz quickly moves toward her. Number 14 bumps into Jazz's chest, but Jazz doesn't fall. Number 14 is forced to pass the ball to an open teammate who still manages to get the shot away. She scores, and puts the Hornets ahead by one point.

Coach Chan calls a timeout with five seconds left in the game.

The Pipers run to the bench. They look at each other nervously.

"What are we going to do?" asks Cindy.

"We've got the ball on the sideline," says Coach Chan. "I want to run *Chop*." He looks at Jazz and Ella. "But only if you two are actually going to run the play."

Ella looks at Jazz. Jazz braces herself. She doesn't know if she's ready for this, but she really wants to win the game. She nods.

"We'll run it," says Ella.

"Good," says Coach Chan. He turns to Joanne.

"When you get the ball, I want you to shoot it right away. Even if you don't think you're open. Everyone else, rebound."

The colour drains from Joanne's cheeks.

I wouldn't want that kind of pressure put on me either, thinks Jazz.

The Pipers run onto the court and get in their spots. Jazz lines up at the top of the key, Ella stands out of bounds, and Joanne stands outside the three-point line. Jazz looks into the stands. All eyes are on the court. With the Pipers down one point, they have to score this basket to win. Number 14 nudges Jazz in the back and Jazz stumbles forward. Jazz shakes it off and gets back in her position.

The referee hands Ella the ball. Ella slaps it and Joanne fakes toward the sideline. Just as Catherine did, Joanne's defender lunges toward the ball. Jazz runs to her position. She jumps and lands with both feet firmly on the ground. Jazz crosses her arms over her chest, careful not to move or lean in either direction.

Behind her, Number 14 yells to her teammate, "Screen coming! Screen coming!"

Joanne's defender hears the warning and looks at Jazz as she runs into the screen. When they make contact, Jazz experiences a wave of relief. Both players stay on their feet. But the moment of relief is short. Ella throws the ball into the air and Joanne runs toward the basket. With Joanne's defender stuck in front of

Jazz, Joanne is wide open. Jazz watches the ball float through the air toward Joanne's shaky hands.

Jazz turns. As the ball touches Joanne's hands, Jazz runs toward the basket. Joanne awkwardly shoots the ball at the basket. The ball hits the backboard and bounces away from the rim. The Hornets' bench stands to celebrate.

Before Jazz has time to think, she's flying through the air with her arms stretched out in front of her.

Jazz catches the rebound.

The crowd goes silent.

Jazz lands and quickly jumps back up again. She shoots the ball just before the horn goes off. The ball hits the backboard and bounces toward the front of the rim. It hits the inside of the rim with a clank. Jazz clamps her eyes shut. She doesn't want to see the ball fall away from the basket.

She doesn't want to lose the game.

Suddenly, the crowd roars. Jazz opens her eyes just in time to see the ball fall through the mesh of the hoop.

Amazed, Jazz looks up at the scoreboard. With no time left on the clock, the Pipers are up by one point.

They've won the championship!

Suddenly, everything moves at once. Teammates are tackling Jazz with hugs and screams. The crowd is cheering wildly.

Jazz can barely think. She looks around. The Hornets' players are looking at the floor, subdued.

"We should do our cheer and shake their hands before we celebrate," Jazz says to her teammates.

The Pipers put their hands together and cheer for the Hornets. Then Jazz leads the team in the end-of-game handshake with the opposing team.

When Jazz gets to the end of the line, she meets Catherine. Catherine hesitates for a moment, but then firmly shakes Jazz's hand.

"Maybe next year we'll get the chance to play against each other in the finals," offers Jazz.

Catherine smiles slightly and nods, letting go of Jazz's hand.

Before Jazz can turn around, she's being lifted into the air by Joanne. "Thank you! Thank you! Thank you!" Joanne says.

It is the most emotion Jazz has ever seen Joanne express. Coach Chan walks onto the court and holds the championship trophy high. Everyone cheers.

Jazz sees Cindy out of the corner of her eye. The two girls look at one another for a moment, but neither says anything.

"You were so good!" says Jazz's mom, running up to her. "Who knew my daughter was so good? And your new friend Ella? I don't know much about basketball, but I like the way she plays."

Jazz looks through the crowd and sees Adam give Ella a hug so big it lifts her off her feet. He spins her in a circle. Jazz walks over to them, smiling.

Ella gives Jazz a high-five. "Awesome rebound!"

"Can I hug you, Jazz?" asks Adam excitedly. "I'd really like to hug you. But I don't know if you want me hugging you in public."

"What do you mean?"

"You may not know this, but I'm not very popular," says Adam. "I don't know why. Maybe you can tell me. That is, if you still want to be friends with me now that the season's over."

Jazz rolls her eyes. "You can hug me, but don't pick me up. Joanne already did that."

Adam gives Jazz a big hug. He pulls back. "Well?"

"Well, what?" asks Jazz.

"Did you have fun?"

Jazz looks at the trophy and around the gym. They'll announce the Most Valuable Player award soon, but Jazz doesn't care if she gets it. Basketball has changed so much for her in the last few weeks, it probably won't ever be exactly like it was before. But Jazz thinks that maybe whatever basketball means to her now could be good, too.

"Well," she says with a smile. "It was a good start."